THE BODY IN THE VOLVO

"The humor is good natured, the plot packs a surprise at the end, and there is a lovely romance between two nice people who don't realize they are attracted to one another."

The Washington Post Book World

"Good work from Beck, whose stories get better all the time."

The Kirkus Reviews

"A cast of artful characters delicately sprinkled with humor ... A whodunit that was delightful to read."

Mystery News

THE BODY IN THE VOLVO

K. K. Beck

IVY BOOKS • NEW YORK

Ivy Books
Published by Ballantine Books
Copyright © 1987 by K. K. Beck

Library of Congress Catalog Card Number: 87-15938

ISBN 0-8041-0371-2

This edition published by arrangement with Walker and Company

All the characters and events portrayed in this story are fictitious.

Manufactured in the United States of America

First Ballantine Books Edition: August 1989

CHAPTER

1

Cosmo Sweeney stood in the middle of the shop, one arm around his nephew Charles, the other sweeping in a great arc. "Here it is, kid," he said. "Yours. All yours." His gesture took in a wide expanse of concrete splotched with oil, racks of jumbled tools, a garbage can full of soiled shop rags, and several cars with their hoods up. Along the walls various automotive body parts were stacked haphazardly, and gaskets and fan belts hung on hooks.

"I really appreciate it, Uncle Cosmo," said Charles. "But are you sure you want to go through with it? Maybe your employees would have liked the business."

"Those bums? Forget it. None of them is smart enough to run this place worth a damn. It's hard getting good help, believe me. No one wants to work anymore. You'll have to ride 'em, really ride 'em." Cosmo smiled. "Course I don't want to work anymore myself, do I?" He laughed the carefree laugh of a man who'd just come into a great deal of money.

Charles couldn't remember Uncle Cosmo ever having

been so relaxed, so pleasant, and so generous. But then, Uncle Cosmo had just won the Washington State lottery. He'd been the first winner in five weeks, and his winnings, on a one dollar Lotto ticket, had been about six million dollars, payable in hefty annual chunks for thirty years. At the televised news conference following his big win, Uncle Cosmo had leaned into a brace of microphones and declared: "I quit. I know a lot of these big winners say nothing'll ever change in their lives, but I plan a few changes, you better believe it. My wife and I are going to find a sunny beach somewhere, and I'll never turn a wrench again."

"You know, Charles," said Uncle Cosmo now, "you're the only one in this family who ever showed much interest in this business, so naturally I thought of you, seeing as they fired you up at the university after all those years you went to school."

"I wasn't fired, Uncle Cosmo," said Charles patiently. "I just didn't get tenure." He was a very handsome man, tall, with dark hair and brows, intelligent gray eyes, a straight, strong nose, and a firm, pleasant mouth.

"Here," said Uncle Cosmo, plunging through the shop and into the front office. "Let me show you the layout." The office consisted of a couple of desks and a file cabinet, a counter, and beyond it a small waiting area with a green plastic couch. "I'm sure you'll pick it up fast. Managed right, this place could be a little gold mine. A real little gold mine.

"These here are the work orders, you know, the invoices, and the books. Let me tell you about the bookkeeper, Mrs. Aldrich. Take my advice and get rid of her. That's what the IRS told me after that audit, but I never had the nerve. She was in the Eastern Star with my mother-in-law. Anyway, she comes in once a week. I just throw all the paperwork in this bin here and she sorts it out.''

Uncle Cosmo rummaged around vaguely with some papers on the surface of a battered old army surplus desk. "Now, this desk is the nerve center of the whole operation. You gotta keep on top of this paperwork or you'll get completely snowed under.'' Stacks of papers with greasy thumbprints sat in piles.

"Here's the checkbook,'' Uncle Cosmo slapped a large volume, "and there's one for the tax and license account around here somewhere. You gotta take out for payroll tax, social security, federal withholding, Labor and Industries, and of course the sales tax. You'll figure it out.

"Gee, I wish I could stick around and help you learn the ropes, but I'm anxious to hit that beach. Don't worry, though, the boys'll know what to do. And you spent enough time here yourself to get the general drift. You'll pick it up.''

Charles had worked for Uncle Cosmo on and off all through high school and college, and during his postgraduate years too. It had worked out well. Uncle Cosmo's shop, on Roosevelt Way in Seattle, a long street of automotive businesses, was close to the University of Washington campus. And Charles had enjoyed the work and enjoyed fooling around with cars. But he'd never given much thought to how the business worked. He supposed, however, that it didn't take a Ph.D. to run a simple operation like this. And Charles had a Ph.D. Now, with his academic career in a shambles, thanks to the tenure committee and its chairman, the despicable Roland Bateman, the idea of being handed a going concern and running it seemed rather attractive.

And if I don't like it, thought Charles, *I can always sell it*. It really was awfully nice of Uncle Cosmo to just sign it over to him. Charles felt a little guilty about this thought, so he said, "You could always sell it, you know. You don't have to give it to me."

"Aw, forget it," said Uncle Cosmo. "I haven't got the time. I'm getting out of here fast. Who wants the aggravation? Besides, I always liked you.

"Now I've had the lawyer draw it all up. It's here somewhere." Uncle Cosmo produced a legal document from beneath a parts catalog. "Says it's all yours. 'Course there are a few debts, but plenty of assets too, and good income potential. Just sign right here."

Charles thought for a minute that perhaps he'd better have a lawyer look it over, but it seemed churlish. After all, Uncle Cosmo had put thirty years into the business, and he was giving it to him outright. Charles took the pen from Uncle Cosmo's hand and signed the two copies. The men shook hands, and then Uncle Cosmo said, "Boy, I can't wait to get the hell out of this place. Here I was, every night 'til eight, every weekend, every holiday, with your aunt hollering at me on the phone to come home and the customers all over me. Thirty years of sheer hell and now I'm a free man." He slapped Charles on the back and said, "It's all yours, kid. All yours."

Charles began to wonder just how much the business would fetch if it were sold. He remembered vaguely seeing ads in the paper of businesses for sale and imagined there were brokers who handled this sort of thing. But he'd better wait until Uncle Cosmo had left for the Bahamas. It would be more tactful.

"Oh, we need a couple of witnesses on this thing," said

4

Uncle Cosmo, frowning at the document. "I hear the boys coming in now."

He flipped an intercom switch on his desk and yelled into it. "Hey guys, come on in and meet the new boss.

"They're great guys," he said to his nephew, "but you gotta keep on their asses all the time."

Three mechanics in blue coveralls trooped into the office. It had been some years since Charles had worked for his uncle, and the place had always had a high turnover, but Charles recognized one of them, a fat, bald, middle-aged man with a kindly face.

"You remember Bud," said Uncle Cosmo. "He's been with me for years. I just turned the place over to my nephew here. Say, sign this, will you? We need a couple of witnesses."

Bud signed and turned the pen over to a young, raw-boned man whose embroidered name on the coveralls said *Steve*. "What kind of shit is this?" said Steve querulously to Charles. "Do you know anything about cars? You're that nephew who's a professor, aren't you? That's just great. A professor. Jesus Christ."

"Don't mind Steve," said Uncle Cosmo. "He's always real irritable. But he's a fine mechanic."

"You're damn straight I am," said Steve belligerently, signing the document with a stabbing, angry motion. "And I want all my parts ready when I get the job and a clean shop and no bullshit."

Charles tried to phrase some sort of response to this outburst, but the other men seemed to be ignoring Steve so he decided to do the same.

"I'll make some coffee," said Bud cosily. "I'm kind of in charge of the coffee around here."

Uncle Cosmo stared down at his hands. "Damn!" he

said jubilantly. "I'll know it's true when I get the grease finally worn away from under these fingernails."

Charles introduced himself to the third mechanic, a pleasant-looking young man with a thin face and a receding hairline. Only two signatures had been required to witness.

"This is Phil," said Uncle Cosmo. "Real good on wiring and charging problems.

"Okay, you guys. Get back to work. That Chevy's been sitting here for a week. What am I going to tell the customer?" He slapped his forehead. "What am I talking about? It's not my problem. Well, so long." And with that, Uncle Cosmo walked out of Cosmo's Car Center without looking back.

"What am *I* going to tell the customer?" asked Charles.

Bud shrugged. "Tell 'em we had parts problems," he said, fussing around the coffee machine.

The other mechanics disappeared into the back, and Charles began to explore the desk. He was sure he'd be able to whip things into shape. He'd always thought Uncle Cosmo ran a kind of tacky operation. Smoother work at the counter, a more genteel atmosphere—maybe some plants—and the customers would come pouring in. That was the problem with the car repair business, thought Charles. Poor image. He'd work on that aspect and let the mechanics do their work. Things should work out beautifully.

The phone rang. Bud hovered around, nodding encouragingly, while Charles took the call.

"Cosmo's Car Center."

"Where the hell's Cosmo?"

"We're under new management," said Charles briskly. "Can I help you?"

"New management, eh? Well, anything would be an

6

improvement," said an angry, high-pitched male voice. "My car still won't run right. It makes a little teeny crackly sound when I go around a corner. And between twenty and thirty, when I switch gears, I hear a little buzzing sound, like a wasp. And the cigarette lighter still takes too long to get hot. It's very annoying."

"Well, bring it back down here," said Charles. "We want you to be happy. Now let's see . . ." Bud handed him an appointment book. "How about Wednesday?"

Bud watched as he wrote down the customer's name. "Oh him," said Bud, sipping coffee, after Charles had hung up. "Mr. Comeback. Your uncle would have told him to go to hell. He's always bitching. Just ignore him."

"Well, if there's something wrong with his car—" began Charles.

"There's never anything wrong with his car," said Bud. "When he comes in we'll give it a test-drive and then wall-job it."

"Wall-job it?"

"Park it by the wall for a few hours and give him a bill when he gets back. Give him some story."

"You mean Uncle Cosmo wasn't running an honest shop?" Charles was shocked.

Bud shrugged. "When there's nothing wrong with the car, what's the point of working on it?"

He squinted past the counter and through the front window. "Oh, here's Gloria." He leaned over to the intercom and switched it on. "Here she comes, boys," he said. "Gloria's a parts runner," he explained to Charles.

A pert little blond carrying a huge cardboard box struggled into the shop. When she had staggered to the counter and put down her box, Charles could see she had a spectacular body packed into tight jeans and a sleazy-looking lace blouse, cut low. A small gold cross nestled between her breasts.

The sound of wrenches hitting concrete was followed by the reappearance of the two mechanics from the back. They lounged around the coffee machine and leered at Gloria.

Gloria handed Charles a computer printout. "Here's the bill," she said in a hard little voice.

"Fine." Charles tried to sound knowledgeable. "I trust we have an account with you."

"Sorry," said Gloria. "It's payment up front for Cosmo's. That's our policy. It comes to one hundred thirty-five dollars and ninety-eight cents."

Charles found the checkbook and wrote her a check. He wasn't a signatory on the account, but he figured he could take care of that before the check cleared. And he remembered what Steve had said about wanting his parts available.

"Remember," said Gloria, looking dubiously at the check, "it's three bounces and then it's strictly cash. You got one to go."

Gloria left, and Steve and Phil drifted back to work. Bud, however, lingered.

"Isn't there something you can do?" said Charles pointedly. Bud looked a little hurt, but he said, "Well, the uniform man comes today. I guess I can go count the shop rags."

"How about working on a car? Haven't we got enough cars in the shop?"

Bud looked thoughtful. "Well, after I count the shop rags maybe I could do that brake job on the Buick."

"Fine," said Charles. "You do that."

Further examination of Uncle Cosmo's desk produced what appeared to be the books. Charles opened up a long, plastic-covered ledger and saw pages of spidery numbers in columns, the work of Mrs. Aldrich, no doubt. Comments had been written in the margins, rather an unusual bookkeeping practice, he thought. He read some of them.

"Missing invoice number. People will think you're skimming." Another said, "Petty cash wrong again. Keep your hands out of there. I called the discrepancy an owner's draw." A third, some pages later, read, "There's $125.93 I can't account for. I've done it over and over and it didn't add up, so I stuck it in charitable contributions."

Grinding his teeth, Charles decided he'd better get rid of Mrs. Aldrich, just as his uncle had suggested. In the yellow pages he found a firm of accounting temporaries. He called up and requested a bookkeeper immediately. A knowledgeable eye on the books should give him a clear picture of the state of the business. The woman at the agency sounded very encouraging. "We'll send you someone right away," she said. "Miss Snow. A real sharp pencil."

The uniform man arrived, and Bud made him a cup of coffee. "Gotta keep friendly with him," he said in an aside to Charles. "He tells us what's going on in the trade."

Fred, the uniform man, informed them that the place up the street had fifteen cars in the shop and was booked up a week in advance. Also that the used car lot on the corner had been indicted for violations of Federal Trade Commission regulations. "The old bait and switch in their advertising," mused Fred.

"Say, you're the new owner, huh? Well, we'll get you suited up too. Large, I guess, and your name on the pocket, that's free. You know, you'll have to do a lot of wrenching yourself, or this place'll drive you to the poor house.'' He shook his head. ''I've seen plenty of shops go down the tube because the owner didn't spend enough time wrenching.''

Steve emerged from the back. ''We don't have any fucking hand cleaner,'' he announced vehemently.

''Okay, okay,'' said Fred. ''I'll get you another bottle.''

''If we bought it by the case, we wouldn't run out,'' snarled Steve.

''Cosmo always said it was too expensive.''

''The trouble with Cosmo was he never could see the big picture,'' said Steve. ''We'll use it up eventually.''

''There is a quantity discount,'' said Fred. ''I got a case out in the truck. I'll go get it.''

''Okay, put it on our account,'' said Charles when Fred returned. Charles attempted to sound as if he were in charge.

''Forget it,'' said Fred as he gathered up a bundle of greasy coveralls. ''It's cash up front for Cosmo's. We got enough rubber checks out of this place to start a retread business.''

Charles ground his teeth again. ''Well, we're changing bookkeepers. I'm sure we'll get things smoothed out.''

''Fine. Until then, cash up front. Let's see, with the uniforms and the hand cleaner that's sixty-two dollars. How many shop rags you got this week, Bud?''

''Two hundred and twenty-nine.''

Fred shook his head ruefully. ''Where do you guys hide 'em? I delivered two hundred and fifty last week.''

''We need more shop rags,'' said Steve. ''How the fuck can I work without enough shop rags?'' He slammed the door, then yelled from behind it, ''If I don't get more shop rags, I'm walking.''

''Add some rags to our order,'' said Charles. He prepared to write a check, but Fred said, "No. I mean real cash."

"Petty cash is over there," said Bud, indicating a metal box. Charles counted out thirty-two dollars and made up the rest from his own wallet.

Bud finally drifted back into the shop area when Fred left, and Charles answered the phone. A customer wanted to know if his car was ready.

Gingerly, Charles stepped back into the shop. Phil and Steve were hard at work. Bud was petting a dog and chatting with someone at the alley entrance. "Come on over here, Charles," said Bud. "Meet Gary. Upholstery man. Does great work." Gary waved.

"Is Mr. Blaine's car ready?" said Charles.

"You mean that green pig?" sneered Steve. "As ready as it gets. That car is pathetic. You tell the customer if it doesn't get proper care it's going to blow a head gasket. I just poked around in there and did what he wanted, but the son-of-a-bitch was too fucking cheap to have it done right."

"Just tell me if it's finished," said Charles.

"Yeah. It's finished."

Charles picked up the phone extension in the shop. "You can come by right away," said Charles. He hoped Mr. Blaine would bring cash so he could buy himself lunch today. Blaine said he'd be over in a few minutes.

"Okay," said Charles. "Where's the car?"

Bud reluctantly broke off his chat with the upholstery man and led Charles into the alley and to the lot at the side of the building. Blaine's car was penned in behind an old Volvo.

"Move that Volvo, will you," said Charles, "and get Blaine's car out front."

"That's funny," said Bud thoughtfully. "I thought that Volvo was one of the cars the city towed away."

"What? You mean the city towed away customers' cars?"

"No. Just a bunch of junkers your uncle had. Parts cars and stuff. They were all parked in the alley and a while back the city came and yellow-tagged all of them. Cosmo was going to move them, but I guess he never got around to it, what with his big win and all, so I figured the city just towed them."

"Well, hadn't we better get them back?"

Bud shrugged. "Not worth it. Costs too much to bail them out. We'd pretty much stripped them all. This Volvo here ran though."

"Well that's good news." Charles's jaw was clenched. "It means we can get it out of the way and get Blaine's car delivered. I'd like to take in a little money around here so I can keep all you good fellows on the payroll."

Charles left Bud to the chore. Back in the office he discovered a dour-looking young woman in a sweater and long, shapeless skirt. She wore a down jacket and scuffed Earth shoes. He imagined she drove an older foreign car.

"Can I help you?" he asked politely. Thank God there were a few customers around. So far the place had seemed like one giant overhead.

"City inspector," said the woman with a thin smile. She held out a business card on cheap paper with her name written on it by hand, a touch Charles found pathetic.

"What are you doing here?" he asked.

"Oh, come on," she said. "I've been around and around with you people. I'm here to see whether you've complied and put in that handicapped bathroom yet. It's got to be wide enough to accommodate a wheel chair, as well as

12

have proper handrails installed. We've been through all this.''

"I'm the new owner," said Charles helplessly. "I'm afraid I don't know anything about it.''

While she rummaged in a cheap plastic briefcase for some papers, Charles took another call. "I need my car fixed. Is Phil there?'' a woman's voice asked.

"Yes, he is. Would you like an appointment?''

"Not with you. Phil works on my car. After work. Can I talk to him?''

"No," said Charles. "He works for me. He's not supposed to be moonlighting. I'll be glad to make an appointment for you, and we'll take care of it. Phil can do the work. What seems to be the problem?''

"Never mind," said the caller, and hung up.

The city inspector produced some smudgy-looking photocopies. "Here are copies of the code. They apply to all auto repair shops. In fact to any facility serving the public.'' She began to circle pertinent paragraphs with a felt-tip pen.

"Excuse me," said Charles, and stepped into the shop, closing the door behind him.

"No moonlighting," he screamed at the mechanics.

"Well, Cosmo always let us take on a little extra work," said Phil nervously.

"No moonlighting," repeated Charles. "How the hell can I make any money running an answering service for you guys?''

Bud, who was sorting through a box of spark plugs and chatting with a couple of dark men with a lot of gold in their teeth and around their necks, spoke up. "But Cosmo always said we could pick up a few jobs.''

"Cosmo's gone. I'm here. And who are these guys?''

"This is Fernando and Carl. From up the street. They own that foreign car place. Hi-Tech Auto. We call them the Corsican brothers."

"We're not really Corsican," said one of them in a strange accent. "How many cars you got in shop today? Business slow by us."

"That's cause you're fucking slimeballs and the word is out," sneered Steve from underneath a car. The Corsican brothers muttered in a foreign language and gestured violently in a vaguely Mediterranean way.

At least, thought Charles, Steve worked while he bitched. He turned to Bud. "How are the brakes coming on that Buick?" he said testily.

"Just fine," said Bud amiably.

"Well, what are you doing with spark plugs if it's a brake job?"

"Hmm? Oh. Thought I better just straighten these out. They're getting kind of messy."

"Forget the spark plugs. Do the brakes," said Charles. "But first, move that Volvo. Blaine is arriving any minute. Then come back and help me write up the work order. I trust someone remembers what, if anything, was done on the car."

"I couldn't find the keys to that Volvo," said Bud. "And you know, that car smells awful."

When Charles returned to the counter, the inspector was taking a tape measure out of her briefcase. "Things will go easier for you if you're cooperative. Now please pay attention to what I have to say."

"I'm trying to run a business," said Charles, exasperated.

"Well if *that's* your attitude," she said huffily.

"Can't we make an appointment and do this later? I have a customer coming in any moment now to pick up a car," Charles began to sort through a shoebox full of keys. Bud came and joined him and then started going through a key rack by the door.

"I'm going to write this up and cite you," said the inspector. "Where's the bathroom?"

"Right through there," said Bud helpfully. "I'm afraid it's not too clean."

"I'll come with you," said Charles, forgetting about the keys and following the woman. "I'm sorry you got us at a bad time," he began plaintively. "I just took over the business." He gave her a nice smile, the kind he had given Dr. Bateman's wife at that ill-fated faculty party.

The inspector thawed a little. "Well, seeing as you're new I'll give you twenty days to comply." She stepped over the case of hand cleaner and went into the bathroom.

As he passed back through the shop, Charles heard Steve snarling. "And *now* we've got some faggot professor running things."

"I don't think he's a faggot," Bud said mildly. "He just tried to follow some broad into the can."

Charles left the inspector to her measuring and went back to the counter. A man identifying himself as Mr. Blaine stood there with his wallet open.

"We just have to move a few cars and we'll be right with you," Charles said. He flipped on the intercom. "Move that Volvo. Hot wire it or push it, I don't care. Just move it, and get Mr. Blaine's car out of there."

The intercom crackled back. "When Blaine shows up, tell that fucking cheapskate the engine'll go if he doesn't have a valve job right away," said Steve's voice.

"Excuse me," said Charles, rushing into the back. "You big jerk, the customer heard you," he hissed to Steve on his way out the back entrance and into the lot.

Phil and Bud, having put a jack under the front end to compensate for the locking steering, were trying to push the car now. Charles took Bud's place and told Bud to write up a bill for Mr. Blaine.

"This car *does* smell terrible," said Charles as he strained alongside Phil. They pushed the Volvo into the shop. "Better check the trunk. It seems to be coming from there."

Now that Blaine's car was freed, Phil drove it around to the front of the shop. Charles rejoined Bud at the counter, where Mr. Blaine was going over his bill.

A uniformed police officer had now come into the lobby. Bud looked up from his calculator. "This is Officer Carelli. He wants to talk to you."

"Hi," said the policeman. "Understand you took over from Cosmo. He's always been a big help to us, so I imagine I can count on you too. Time to take out an ad in the patrolman's newsletter. How about if I put you down for a quarter page? We can just take the copy from your business card."

"Well, how much does it cost?" Charles asked warily.

"Three hundred dollars. And you get a sticker that says you helped out. Goes right on your windshield. Kind of handy if you ever get stopped." The policeman winked.

"I don't know," began Charles.

"Well, you think about it," said the officer with a little frown. "While I'm here I'll do a little checking. See how secure the place is. Cosmo tells me none of these tools are insured."

Charles wondered if this was some kind of shakedown. Academic life hadn't prepared him for the realities of business. Maybe he should bribe that inspector too. He

16

had just noticed her taking Polaroid pictures of the bathroom, presumably for later use in court.

Meanwhile, he wondered what to say to Mr. Blaine about Steve's remark on the intercom. He coughed delicately. "I'm sorry about that mechanic," said Charles. "He's a little volatile."

"I *told* Cosmo I didn't need a valve job," said Blaine. "And that blatant little outburst isn't going to change my mind. I know what I need. I know a lot about cars."

Steve had strolled into the office and was wiping his hands on a shop rag. He threw it into the wastebasket. So that's where they went, thought Charles.

"Yeah?" said Steve. "Well, if you know so fucking much about cars, why don't you work on them yourself? That car needs a valve job." He turned to Charles. "If I were you I'd write on the work order that without further repairs you don't guarantee the owner's personal safety."

"Go back into the shop," said Charles. "And stay away from the customers. Please."

Steve shrugged and mercifully sauntered back into the shop.

"I'm so sorry, Mr. Blaine," began Charles.

The city inspector came by and set an official-looking document on the counter on her way out. "You've got twenty days to comply. That wall's got to be moved three feet south."

"Thank you for being so understanding," said Charles, with another nice smile.

Leaving Bud to finish up with Mr. Blaine, Charles went back into the shop area. When that accountant showed up, he was going to have her go over the whole thing and tell him what the business was worth. Then he'd put Cosmo's Car Center on the market and get back to sending out resumés. Uncle Cosmo's winning the lottery and giving him the business had seemed providential. A sign that academic life was not for him. Now he wasn't so sure. Maybe he could still get that interview in South Dakota.

Surveying the shop, he toyed briefly with the idea of firing Steve. He understood that in the private sector you could simply fire someone. It wasn't like the university, where you had to get a committee together to cobble up a bunch of excuses. But what difference did it make anyway? Bateman had got him canned just as surely as if he'd walked over to him and said, "You're through. Pack up your tools and go."

Charles braced himself for making this speech to Steve and went over to him. Steve was wrenching away, cursing softly at the car. He seemed to reserve his higher volume for humans.

"Steve," began Charles. But he stopped. It occurred to him that, unpleasant as Steve was, he seemed to be doing most of the work around the place. Bud had spent the morning gossiping and making coffee and puttering around, not unlike an older, tenured professor. Of course Phil seemed all right. He seemed the most normal of the trio.

Bud bustled back into the shop. "How you doing, Phil?" he said in a kindly manner. "Did you take your medication today?"

"Oh, sure," said Phil, examining the Volvo. "This trunk lock is completely frozen."

"That's good," said Bud. "Don't want you to go off the rails again, do we? Isn't it nice they can keep your condition under control with medication?"

Charles decided he'd better not fire Steve right away. He went over and inspected the Volvo. It was a 140 model, full of rust, and the windshield had been shattered.

There was plenty of glass in the front seat. "Well, take a chisel to it," he said. "There's something foul in that trunk. Maybe a couple of salmon or something. What's the story on this car anyway?"

"Just one of Cosmo's little projects," said Bud, browsing around with a chisel. "He was going to build it up, paint it, and sell it."

"That car's a piece of shit," commented Steve.

"Is Blaine gone?" asked Charles.

"Yes," said Bud. "He paid his bill and left."

"I guess we'll never see him again." Charles glared at Steve.

"So what?" said an unremorseful Steve. "He's too fucking cheap. We need better customers."

"Yeah, a classy guy like you belongs in an upscale shop," Charles said sarcastically and went back into the office.

A young woman stood there, carrying a wicker basket. She was rather arty looking, with long dark hair parted in the middle and done up at the back in a knot. She wore large silver loops in her ears and gazed at him soulfully with big, dark eyes. He gave her his nice smile. The basket looked as if it might contain a kitten.

"I'm Sylvia Snow," she said. "From the accounting service."

Great, thought Charles. *This is the sharp pencil they send over. She looks like something from a coffee house, circa 1962.* "Well I'm glad you're here," he said doubtfully. "I've just taken over this business, and I'd like to know what shape it's in."

"Fine," said the young woman, removing an outer garment resembling a blanket that seemed to be woven out of yak hair.

19

"The circumstances are rather unusual," began Charles. He explained how Uncle Cosmo had handed over the business to him that morning. "But I really don't know where I stand. And I have reason to believe the bookkeeper was less than efficient."

Miss Snow took a heavy-looking electronic calculator with a paper roll attached to it out of her basket and set it on the counter. "Well, I presume you have some kind of records?"

Charles furnished her with what Uncle Cosmo had shown him.

"What about tax records, payroll records, bank accounts?"

"I don't really know where anything is," said Charles apologetically. He indicated the filing cabinet. "Dig around and see what you can find."

Miss Snow said, "I imagine you'd like to know how much the business is worth and how much income you can expect from it."

"Yes, that's it exactly," said Charles. "Why don't you take this other desk here?"

Officer Carelli strolled back into the shop. "That alarm system of yours needs upgrading," he said. "In fact, I don't think it's functional. But the wires on the glass and that sticker ought to fool the bad guys."

The phone rang. "This is the Better Business Bureau," said a cold, hard voice. "You haven't responded to the complaint we have against you."

"I'll call you back," said Charles, slamming down the phone. He made his hand into a fist and pounded it on the counter. "If it wasn't for that goddamned Professor Bateman I wouldn't be here," he said.

Just then the intercom crackled to life. Bud's voice came into the room. "I hope that cop's gone," he said.

"Because we got big trouble back here. Better take a look."

Charles, followed by Officer Carelli, went back into the shop. Bud and Phil were standing by the Volvo with its trunk lid now opened. Bud looked his usual pleasant self, but Phil, holding a chisel and leaning on the side of the car, looked decidedly green.

Inside the trunk, folded up in the fetal position, was the body of a silver-haired man in a tweed jacket with suede patches on the elbows. It was the jacket that Charles recognized first.

"My God," he said. "It's Dr. Bateman."

CHAPTER
2

own. You'll find one had here a crafty pillory. Th
'o an excellent resin
ally a-s-sar

C HARLES had last seen Dr. Bateman alive and well about two weeks before. It was with some trepidation that Charles had accepted Bateman's invitation to lunch at an excellent downtown restaurant. He had tried, however, to dismiss the horrible, hollow feeling of impending doom. After all, if, as certain whispers and rumors from the department had led him to believe, Dr. Bateman was about to let the ax fall, why would he invite his victim to a nice lunch?

It must mean that his career had somehow been saved. Maybe Charles had been paranoid. Maybe the furtiveness of his colleagues, the unsettling way conversation turned to embarrassed silence when he entered the department office, had all been coincidence.

Bateman was already ensconced at a cosy table in the dimly lit room. It was paneled in dark wood, and there were some tasteful prints on the wall and soft carpeting underfoot.

"Ah," he said smoothly. "Young Carstairs. Do sit

down. You'll find the food here is really excellent. They do an excellent thing here with medallions of veal. I'd really recommend it." Charles watched Dr. Bateman going over the menu with a scholarly air.

Actually, Dr. Bateman looked as much like a stereotypical professor as anything Central Casting could have arranged. His spiky, silvery hair was decently cut, but never seemed to stay combed down, as if, during knotty intellectual problems, Dr. Bateman twisted it in concentration. His suit, though obviously expensive and of fine tweed, hung baggily on his burly form, and he favored rather lumpy-looking knit ties.

Dr. Bateman's florid face, with the comfortable, puffy look of one who enjoyed food and drink, was marked by keen gray eyes, fierce silver brows, and a mouth that, at the moment, was pushed into a little rosebud shape, as it so often was when he was contemplative or when he was phrasing some cutting remark to be delivered in a falsely jocular manner.

"The veal sounds fine," said Charles. He wasn't about to disagree with Dr. Bateman. If he had suggested Beef-A-Roni, Charles would have acted thrilled at the prospect.

"There. Well then, that's settled. And I'll order a half carafe of wine. But shall we have a little something first? A sherry perhaps?"

"Sounds perfect."

When the sherry arrived, Charles imagined Dr. Bateman would get to the point. Instead, he maundered on about the etymology of the word sherry and the town of Jerez, Spain, then made a transition to his own sabbatical year in the south of France. What Dr. Bateman had been studying there no one in the department ever quite knew, and Dr.

Bateman's comments now weren't illuminating on this point either.

Finally, after soup, during which Charles listened politely to Dr. Bateman's views on a new proposal to revise some procedural aspects of the Academic Senate, the veal arrived. Now at last they must get to the reason for their meeting.

Dr. Bateman cut into his veal with surgical precision and inspected the exposed flesh anxiously. Apparently its pinkness met with his approval, for he allowed a wintry smile to come over his features. "I suppose you're wondering why I asked you here today."

Charles smiled nervously. "Well, yes, I had."

"You see," said Dr. Bateman solemnly, "I like you." Charles felt himself beginning to relax, and the other man continued. "I wanted to tell you personally about your future in the department." He paused and chewed.

"I'd like to hear about that," said Charles finally.

Dr. Bateman swallowed. "I'm sorry to say that there is no future for you in the department. Your request for tenure has been denied. On my recommendation."

Charles looked down at his plate. How was he ever going to get through the whole meal? A wave of nausea shuddered through him. "I'm sorry to hear that," he said feebly, looking around the table for something to drink. The half carafe of wine had, after Dr. Bateman had poured himself out a healthy slug, still some wine in it. Charles grabbed the thing by its neck and emptied the contents into his own glass.

"But I thought it would be so *cold* to just send you something in writing," said Dr. Bateman. "Although of course you will receive official notification. In fact, I think you'll find it waiting in your box after lunch." He dabbed his mouth with a large napkin.

Charles took a deep sip of his wine and sawed away at the veal.

"I suppose you want to know why," said Dr. Bateman smiling.

"Of course," said Charles, although he knew perfectly well why.

"Well, I know the students like you a lot. You have a lot of, what shall we say, *pizzazz*, in the lecture hall. I flatter myself that in my younger days, before I really began to apply myself seriously to academic work, I, too, could wow 'em at the podium."

Charles doubted this.

Dr. Bateman went on after a self-deprecating wave. "But we don't really need *stars* in the department, do we? I mean what do those kids know, anyway? The undergraduates these days," he shuddered, "are a lot of simpleminded mall rats, as I'm sure you'll agree. I'm glad you've amused them, but there is more to the department than *fun*."

"So my lectures were too interesting," said Charles, grinding his molars. "I see. But I've published a lot. Surely you took that into account."

"Published a lot? Oh, no doubt about it. A lot. But it gives one pause, doesn't it? How can a serious scholar publish a lot without a resulting loss in *quality*? Hmm?"

"I guess it depends on how good you are," said Charles, draining the last of his wine.

"Precisely my point," said Dr. Bateman. "Now I'll tell you frankly, these shortcomings could have been overlooked, because I like you so much, if it hadn't been for that abominable 'Abominable Snowman' paper of yours.

I mean, really, it was the smoking gun. You made the department a laughingstock.''

"Well, it wasn't my fault that supermarket tabloid picked it up. And if you *read* my paper, I'm sure you'll recall it wasn't about the Abominable Snowman at all, but about Indian legends concerning the Sasquatch and how they compare with modern sightings of Big Foot, or Sasquatches or whatever you want to call them. It was an analysis of myth and how it applies . . ."

Charles trailed off. Perhaps he had tried to do too much in "Establishing Primary Performance Matrices in Analysis of Social Organization of Hitherto Unclassified Primates of Large Dimensions."

"Let me just say," said Bateman, "that the dean himself brought that lurid headline to my attention. 'New Scientific Proof That Big Foot is for Real. The Big Hairy Guys Want to Be Our Buddies, Claims Prof.' " Bateman quoted it with satisfaction. He looked down at Charles's plate. "But you aren't eating your lunch."

Charles pushed some of the food around on his plate and eyed Dr. Bateman's full wineglass enviously.

"Now of course you can appeal, but I wouldn't advise it." Dr. Bateman waggled a finger at him. "No point coming across like a troublemaker."

"This has been quite a blow," said Charles.

"Oh, don't take it so hard. I'll write you nice recommendations. I may even be able to get you an interview with an old colleague of mine. He's the department chairman at a little four-year liberal arts college somewhere in the Dakotas.

"And of course," Bateman sipped his wine and crumbled bread, "you have a whole year to find something else. I saw the schedule for next quarter. I see they've got

26

you doing the seven A.M. Intro class. That's always a trial, but I'm sure you'll manage. And then you've got that midday senior seminar and the night class in Methods. How do you feel about that?''

"I'm really too stunned to think about next quarter just now."

"I'd advise you to keep your spirits up. No point risking a poor recommendation because of sloppy work while you're a lame duck.''

"Dr. Bateman, I really am in a state of shock. I would hate to think there was anything personal in this decision.'' Dr. Bateman's eyes narrowed over the rim of his wineglass, but Charles plunged on. "I can't really think there's any other justification for denying me tenure. If you've heard any rumors or anything about me, anything that perhaps I could explain . . .'' Charles wondered how far he could go with this line. Dr. Bateman's features were beginning to resemble a mask of rage, so Charles decided to drop it.

"Well,'' said Bateman grimly, "of course a high moral tone and conduct becoming a member of the academic community is important too. But nothing like that had anything to do with the decision of the committee. Of course,'' he continued icily, "if you want to appeal you are at liberty to do so. I do not, however, advise it.''

His face relaxed again. "How about some cheesecake? They do an awfully good cheesecake.''

"No cheesecake,'' said Charles firmly. There were limits. "I really have no appetite after receiving this news.''

"Very well,'' said Dr. Bateman with a scowl. "I guess I won't have any either then.'' He sulked a little, as if it were somehow Charles's fault he was missing dessert. He hailed a waiter and arranged for two coffees and the bill.

Charles was so angry he couldn't bear to look at Dr. Bateman. He looked around the room, where tables of people all seemed to be having terrific lunches. Hysterical laughter came from one table. Another featured an intense and lively discussion. Everyone in the place seemed to be having fun except Charles. And, of course, everyone in the place but Charles probably had a steady job.

When the check came, Dr. Bateman slipped on his half-moon glasses and added up the figures. Charles imagined he was making sure he hadn't been cheated. Bateman looked up at him. "Seeing as we both had the same things," he said, "I guess we can split it straight down the middle. Unless of course you want an extra cup of coffee."

CHAPTER
3

Aᴷᵀᴱᴿ the body was discovered, Charles staggered back into the office and Officer Carelli barked code numbers into his walkie-talkie. Charles turned to Miss Snow, her fingers poised gracefully over the keyboard of her printing calculator, and said apologetically, "I'm afraid there's a dead body in the trunk of a car back there." Then, pale, he sank into a chair.

"My God," said Miss Snow, her brows rising. "Anyone you know?"

"That's the damnedest thing," said Charles. "It's Professor Bateman."

Officer Carelli had now followed Charles into the office. "That's the same guy, huh?"

"I've told you. It's Professor Bateman from the University of Washington."

"But isn't he the one you were just talking about before we rushed back there?" said the officer persistently.

"What? Oh, I may have said something about him. I don't quite remember what."

The policeman turned to Miss Snow. "You were a witness. What was it he said about this Bateman character?"

Miss Snow nodded nervously and looked at Charles with big, solemn, dark eyes. "I remember," she said softly.

"Well! What did he say?" demanded Carelli.

Miss Snow cleared her throat. "He said, as far as I can recall, 'If it weren't for that goddamned Professor Bateman, I wouldn't be here.' "

"Aha!" said Officer Carelli, scribbling this down in a little notebook.

"I'm sorry," Miss Snow said to Charles. "But I do remember your saying that."

"Well don't worry about it," said Charles. "I guess it's no secret I hated Bateman's guts, but that doesn't mean I killed him."

Officer Carelli continued writing, looking up for a moment at Charles with a gleam in his eye.

Soon the police arrived in force, preceded by sirens. A couple of detectives took over and, ignoring everyone but Professor Bateman, piled into the shop area. They seemed to be standing around talking and gossiping, from what Charles could tell. He heard one of them say, "Gee, I thought Volvos were supposed to be such safe cars," and then general laughter. They were joined shortly by more men in plain clothes, one of whom seemed to be a doctor, and by more uniformed officers.

After the initial shock of the discovery had begun to wear off, it occurred to Charles that this development was bad for business.

For one thing, the police had put up a long yellow ribbon around the property. It was marked *Police Line—*

Crime Scene—Do Not Cross. A few people, possibly potential customers, were standing outside the line, peering anxiously into the shop.

Bud bustled out and began to work the line, obviously in his element. He chatted with Gary the upholstery man, Fred, the uniform man, the Corsican brothers, and others whom Charles did not recognize, but who had presumably been drawn to the site by the police sirens. Finally Officer Carelli chased Bud back into the shop. Charles reflected that if he, too, wore a gun maybe he could get Bud away from his chatty rounds and to work.

Soon, however, the police herded the three mechanics into the lobby area, where they sat in a row on the green plastic sofa browsing through ancient magazines, until Bud went into a corner and came up with an old portable television set. He plugged it in, turned it on, and music, eerily dirgelike for the occasion, boomed into the room.

"For God's sake," snapped Charles. "Turn that thing off."

Bud, looking hurt, said, "But Cosmo always let me watch 'As The World Turns.' "

"Cosmo!" said Charles. "We'd better call him. Maybe he'll know how Professor Bateman got into that trunk."

"The way the cops been talking," said Steve, *"you* know more about it than anyone."

"What?" said Charles.

"They were saying you hated this guy's guts and probably wasted him and stuffed him in the trunk of that car." Steve seemed to be eyeing Charles with newfound respect.

"That's ridiculous. If that were true, why would I have insisted the trunk be opened?"

Steve laughed. "The detectives said maybe you forgot it

31

was in there. You know, the absent-minded professor bit.''

Phil, sitting next to him, looked edgy. ''This whole thing is getting me real stressed out,'' he whined. ''How long do I have to stay here?''

''As far as I'm concerned,'' said Charles, ''if you aren't allowed to work back there, you may as well go home.'' Not only did Charles resent paying his mechanics for sitting around, he didn't want Phil's psychotropic medication to wear off.

Bud, who had been looking forlornly at the dead TV screen, chimed in. ''The cops say we have to stay here until they say we can go. Her too.'' He pointed to Miss Snow.

She, however, seemed to be getting on with her work. Her calculator made a rather comforting buzzing noise as she did, and her smooth brow was furrowed in concentration.

Charles called Uncle Cosmo's number. A recording came on. ''Hello, this is Cosmo Sweeney. I'm not here right now, in fact, I've left the country, so if you heard about my big win and want a handout, forget it. You can leave a message at the sound of the tone, but I won't be able to answer you anyway, so why bother? Ha!'' Uncle Cosmo may well have been besieged by various kinds of desperate and crazy people, since his lottery win had received so much publicity. On the chance Uncle Cosmo was still around, and hiding behind the recording, Charles left a message.

''This is your nephew Charles. Please call me at the shop as soon as possible. Something's come up.'' Charles didn't want to say too much more. Uncle Cosmo hated unpleasantness. If Charles had told him about the dead body it would be just like Uncle Cosmo not to get in touch. Anyway, Uncle Cosmo had said he was leaving for the Bahamas. Maybe he was already on his way.

Charles decided that, however Dr. Bateman had come to be stuffed in the trunk of that Volvo, it had happened on Uncle Cosmo's shift and wasn't his, Charles's, responsibility at all. He went back into the shop to tell the detective who seemed to be in charge just that.

A knot of men stood around the trunk of the car. Charles was rather horrified to see Dr. Bateman's arm extended from the trunk. Someone was calmly scraping the fingernails of the white, bloodless hand with a small tool, as if giving the corpse a manicure.

Shuddering, Charles turned his back on the grisly scene and addressed one of the plain clothes policemen, a large, square-jawed man with sandy hair moussed rather elaborately into a style reminiscent of local TV anchor men.

"MacNab. Homicide," said the man. "You must be the professor."

"That's right. Charles Carstairs."

"We were just about to talk to you."

"Well, I thought you should know this is my first day as owner. I've only just got here. My uncle, Cosmo Sweeney, was in charge until, well, just a few hours ago."

MacNab's eyes narrowed. "So you think this is all your uncle's fault?"

"No, not at all." Charles realized he sounded if he were somehow passing the buck to Uncle Cosmo. But, damn it, Uncle Cosmo had been in charge when it happened. "It's just that I can't tell you too much about this, having just arrived. I don't know anything about how the car got here or anything."

"Well, you know something about this Bateman character, don't you?" said MacNab. "Officer Carelli here says he was your worst enemy."

"That's a little dramatic," said Charles. "I wouldn't call him an *enemy* exactly."

"No? What would you call him?" Charles realized that as they were talking MacNab was shifting around so that Charles had to look at the corpse. Really, he thought, does he think I'm going to fall apart at the sight of the corpse, collapse to the ground, and confess? He averted his eyes from the crumpled form and continued. "Dr. Bateman? Well, he was the head of the tenure committee. And I didn't get tenure." Charles tried to look as if this were no big deal.

"You mean he fired you?" said MacNab. A second man, younger and thinner, with prematurely gray hair was listening silently.

"No," said Charles sharply. "I didn't get tenure. It's not exactly the same thing."

"Isn't it?" MacNab paused, gave Charles a heavy-lidded, contemptuous look, and said, "I guess he didn't think you were doing a good job."

"It wasn't that at all," said Charles heatedly. "He may have pretended he didn't like my teaching or my research, but it was all a pretense. He wanted to get rid of me for petty, personal reasons."

"Yeah? Like what?"

Charles knew he was on dangerous ground here, but he also knew that a few questions in the department would bring the whole thing to the surface anyway.

"Oh," said Charles. "He had this idea that his wife and I were . . ." He trailed off, took a deep breath, and began again. "It was ridiculous, of course. There was nothing, well, nothing but that one . . ."

MacNab waited patiently while Charles flailed around, trying to tell his story. Finally he said, "So you were screwing his wife and he found out, huh?"

"Mrs. Bateman. No! It was just, well, once at a faculty party Bateman came into the kitchen and Mrs. Bateman had me backed into a corner by the refrigerator, and he thought . . ." Charles smiled nervously. "You know how these faculty parties get," he added inanely, glancing over at the gray-haired detective, who remained impassive.

"Not really," said MacNab. "Never busted one up for disorderly conduct. But I'll take your word for it they're pretty wild. Professors on the rampage, eh?"

"Professors' wives, anyway," said Charles, ignoring the heavy sarcasm. "Mrs. Bateman is kind of the frisky type. She had the hots for me. What could I do when she jumped me in the kitchen, slap her face?"

"What did you do?"

"Nothing. I mean, we just nuzzled a little, and then her husband walked in. Elizabeth, Mrs. Bateman, that is, is a very attractive woman, and we'd both had a few drinks. But she started it." Charles imagined he sounded like rapists, with whom the detective may have had professional dealings. "Pretended she needed me to help her look for the club soda."

"Well, what happened when her husband caught you two groping around? Was there a scene?"

"Not really. Mrs. Bateman just, um, buttoned up her blouse, and I said I was sorry and I didn't know what I was doing. Actually, I hadn't known it was Dr. Bateman's wife until he showed up and said, 'Let go of my wife.'

"So I said, 'This is your wife?' and he said, 'As if you didn't know,' and she said, 'Darling, why didn't you tell

35

me about this charming young man in your department? Why don't we have him to dinner sometime?' And then she kind of moseyed out of the kitchen, and Dr. Bateman took her home.'' Charles looked thoughtful. ''Things were never the same at work after that.''

''I bet. Did they have you to dinner?''

Charles laughed bitterly. ''Are you kidding? But Elizabeth did call and suggest we have lunch. I was kind of caught off guard, so I said yes, but then I thought better of it and canceled on some pretext. Anyway, Dr. Bateman found a phone message in my box from her. You know, one of those *While You Were Out* things. It said, 'Mrs. Bateman called to say she's sorry you can't make lunch. Call her to reschedule. How about dinner?' ''

Charles sighed. ''That's the whole sordid story. And then he got rid of me and screwed up my career.''

MacNab, who had now made a complete circle so he was standing with his back to the corpse, stepped aside so as to give Charles a clearer view and, watching his reaction, said, ''Plenty of men have been killed for less.''

''But surely you don't think I—'' began Charles, looking at the ceiling rather than at Dr. Bateman's remains.

MacNab interrupted. ''Don't leave town.'' He turned to a uniformed officer. ''See if you can get a hold of this Cosmo character.''

Rather dazed, and surprised to discover he had poured out the whole story of Mrs. Bateman to detective MacNab with apparently very little encouragement, Charles went back into the office. Maybe he should have called a lawyer before he had talked to the police. This was the second time today he had thought too late about consulting a lawyer. The first time was just before he signed the ill-fated paper turning over Cosmo's Car Center to him. The place was nothing but a little shop of horrors.

In the lobby, the three mechanics were watching "As The World Turns," while Miss Snow was hard at work on the books. She looked up at him in an inquiring way, and he said, "I can't believe it. That detective told me not to leave town. Just like in the movies. He said, 'Don't leave town.' "

"Don't tell me about it," said Miss Snow out of the side of her mouth. "Save it for the D.A." Then, burying her face in her hands and suppressing a nervous giggle, she said, "Oh I *am* sorry. It's just that I've always wanted to say that to someone. I know you must be very tense. I didn't mean to joke around."

"God forbid a bookkeeper should have a sense of humor," he replied. "Got any idea where I stand yet? Financially, I mean."

Miss Snow shook her head sadly from side to side. "I'm afraid that the records are in horrible shape. It's a little hard to tell just what has been going on. There's a paper trail, though, and I should be able to put something together in a few days. But I will say that I'm kind of nervous. When records are in such bad shape, it usually indicates the business is too. By the way," she added, "I balanced your checkbook. You're overdrawn."

Charles sighed. The phone rang, and Officer Carelli, who was lingering around the waiting area with one eye on "As The World Turns" and the other rather suspiciously on Charles, picked it up.

"Sorry," he said. "This establishment is closed by order of the Seattle Police Department."

"Oh, honestly," said Charles, exasperated. Before he

knew what he was doing, he had grabbed the receiver, just in time to hear someone at the other end say in a rough, angry voice, "Well that doesn't surprise me a bit. Bunch of crooks if you ask me."

"The police haven't closed us down because of our business practices," said Charles haughtily. "It's only a murder. Nothing to do with your car." Realizing how ridiculous this sounded, he began to backpedal. "That is, I'm sorry for the inconvenience."

"Not as inconvenient as for whoever it was you killed," said the voice. "Now listen, it's about that trans job you people did on my Pontiac. It's completely screwed up and I want you to make it good."

"I don't know anything about it," said Charles. "I've just taken over the business. Bring it in, with your invoice, and we'll take a look at it. When the police let us open again."

"You bet I will," said the angry voice. The caller hung up.

The phone rang again. This time Charles grabbed it before Officer Carelli had a chance.

"Is Phil there? It's about my car."

"Forget it," said Charles testily. "Phil isn't moonlighting any more."

"Who's this? Where's Cosmo?"

"Cosmo's gone, and Phil doesn't moonlight."

"Well, let me talk to him," said the voice, surly and young. "It's Eddie."

Reluctantly, Charles handed the receiver to Phil. "No moonlighting," he hissed at him. "It's Eddie."

"That's right," said Phil into the mouthpiece, looking nervously at Charles. "I can't take on any extra stuff.

Things are real weird here anyway. The cops are here. They found a dead body in the trunk of an old Volvo around here. A 140 with a smashed-in windshield. I'm real stressed out. I was the one that popped the damn trunk open." Phil looked unhappy at the memory.

"Is that Fast Eddie?" said Bud, coming over to the phone. Charles imagined Bud missed his opportunities to chat and gossip now that a police cordon had been thrown up around the place. "Tell him to say hello to Corky. How are things up at Elwood's?"

"All right, all right," said Officer Carelli, grabbing the phone from Phil. "Get off that line. We may need it for police business."

MacNab came into the office now and said to Charles, "Tell us about that car. I understand it's been around for a while. Maybe a week with Dr. Bateman in it, the doc says."

"I don't know anything about it," said Charles. It seemed he had been saying this phrase all morning. "My uncle apparently had a collection of junker cars and that was one of them."

MacNab nodded. "We'll run a make on it."

Bud came over and said, "We all thought it was towed away. When the city took those other cars."

"So you're saying it was towed away and reappeared here with the boss's worst enemy folded up in the trunk?"

"I don't know," said Bud. "It was here, then I think it was gone. Then it was here again. I'm not sure. But it didn't have that damaged windshield when it was here before."

"That's strange," mused Charles. "Why would the windshield be damaged?"

"That's the least of your problems," said MacNab.

"Well one of my main problems right now," said Charles, "is that I'm trying to run a business here. Can't you just take the car and, er, Dr. Bateman, and do whatever it is you have to do somewhere else?"

"We'll be here awhile," said MacNab. "We've got to go through every tool in the place. The doc says one of them may have been the weapon."

Phil, slightly agitated, rose from the couch. "You mean you want to go through my tool box? I don't want anyone going through my tool box. I've got it arranged just the way I want it."

"Phil's very particular about his tools," said Bud.

"I don't know why you're so fucking fussy," snarled Steve. "The Rench-Rite rep is about to repo them anyway."

"I'm paying him something every week," said Phil.

"Yeah, and every week he sells you something new."

"That Rench-Rite rep is real persuasive," said Bud. He turned to MacNab. "I hope you won't get our tools mixed up."

"What difference does it make?" asked MacNab.

"Mechanics generally own their own tools," explained Charles. He knew that some mechanics become obsessive about their tools, and that the mobile tool salesmen who called on repair shops often had compulsive tool buyers get in hock to them. "There should be four sets here. One for each mechanic and one for the shop."

"Oh. Well you guys can come back here with me and tell me what's what."

They all followed MacNab into the shop, Phil wringing his hands.

Officer Carelli now sat down to watch "As The World

Turns" without interruptions, and Miss Snow continued frowning over the books.

"Pretty bad, huh?" ventured Charles.

"Well it's hard to say. You could use some quick cash, though. If this investigation means you aren't going to have any income for a few days, checks drawn on that overdrawn account are going to start bouncing. It could cause some credit problems."

Charles, reflecting on Gloria, the parts runner, and Fred, the uniform man, said, "Too late. From what I can tell, Uncle Cosmo's credit was already shot."

"Still," said Miss Snow, "he seemed to be doing a pretty good volume. Look at all these invoices, just from the past month." She patted a pile of yellow carbon copies. "I'll total these and see how much can go through here a month." She began clacking away at her keyboard. "It could just be a case of bad management. Maybe with a trimmed overhead and better financial practices, this place could be a little gold mine."

"Funny," said Charles, "that's what Uncle Cosmo said this morning. A little gold mine." Could it have been this morning? It seemed he'd been here for days.

"Oh!" said Miss Snow sharply. "Here's an invoice for Dr. Bateman. He was in three weeks ago."

"Let's see that," said Charles. He hadn't known that Dr. Bateman was a customer, although Charles had always handed Uncle Cosmo's business cards around the department. He'd thought Uncle Cosmo needed more business. Of course, if he'd known Uncle Cosmo was as shady as he was beginning to suspect he was, Charles would never have recommended his services to colleagues. Even Dr. Bateman.

Miss Snow handed over the invoice. Dr. Bateman had had his Volkswagen Rabbit tuned here. New cap and rotor, plugs, oil and fuel filter. Idle adjusted. Oil changed. It came to $175.90. Dr. Bateman had put the whole thing on his American Express card.

"I better show this to that detective," said Charles.

"I think this is good news for you," said Miss Snow. "It means you weren't the only association Bateman had with this place." She smiled at him.

Charles smiled back. Miss Snow seemed to want Charles to be innocent. It was the nicest thing that had happened to him all day.

CHAPTER
4

THINGS took a decided turn for the worse a few hours later, however. After what seemed like endless comings and goings of policemen and technicians, MacNab and the man with gray hair came into the office. MacNab, who seemed to be the leader, spoke up.

"We'd like you to come downtown with us, Dr. Carstairs, and make a statement. This is my partner, Detective Lukowski."

Charles didn't like the sound of this at all. "Do I have to?" he said.

"We're sorry for any inconvenience, Dr. Carstairs," said Lukowski.

MacNab interrupted with an impatiently raised hand. "Look," he said. "As far as I'm concerned, we've got probable cause to go right ahead and arrest you without a warrant. It'll be a lot more pleasant for you if you come along with us and tell us what you know right now."

Lukowski shrugged, as if to indicate that his partner was overzealous. Charles looked around the office, where the mechanics and Miss Snow were all staring at him with fascination.

"Of course I'll be glad to help you any way I can," he said in what he hoped sounded like the affable tones of an innocent man and a good citizen. "I'm sure we can clear this all up in no time," he added, meaning that he was sure they could eliminate him as a suspect immediately.

"That's just the way I feel," said MacNab. "Most homicides," he added, "are pretty clear-cut. This might just be one of those cases."

"How long will this take?" asked Charles, imagining hours of grilling beneath cruel lights and the specter of rubber hoses hanging in the air as the two shirt-sleeved detectives ground him down with questioning.

"Like I said," continued MacNab confidently, "most homicides are real clear-cut."

The ride downtown began ominously. Charles was guided into the backseat of a police car. MacNab sat next to the uniformed officer who drove. Lukowski slid into the backseat next to Charles. A chill went through him as the door locks slid implacably down, controlled from the front seat.

Everyone was silent for a while, but as the police car merged onto the freeway, Lukowski leaned over to Charles. "You know," he said, "I took one of your courses when I was at the U. of W."

Charles perked up. Perhaps this Lukowski was one of those college-educated detectives they always had in books. The kind who quoted Jacobean poetry or practiced zen. "I hope you enjoyed it," he said.

Lukowski smiled. "I was only there for a week. I had to drop the class because of a schedule conflict."

"Oh. At least I didn't flunk you. Ha, ha." Charles

heard himself trying to be jocular and sounding like a perfect fool.

They arrived at the Public Safety Building, a hideous thing of purple marble on Third and James Streets, and took the elevator up to the homicide division. Charles hoped the people in the elevator thought he was an expert witness or a friend of the detectives, but nobody seemed to be speculating about him at all.

Soon he found himself in an interview room, a bare but carpeted cubicle with a Formica table and chairs. Across one wall, recognizable from research in his field that Charles had done in the past, was a mirror that from its strange sheen was clearly the two-way kind. He wondered who, if anyone, was sitting behind that mirror, and shuddered. The whole process was so undignified.

Surprisingly, Lukowski, who never had seemed to be in charge, began. "Now I'm going to suggest something, Doctor, and I hope you don't mind. I was thinking if we tape record our conversation here, then there's no danger of anyone being misquoted later. Is that okay with you? Strictly routine, and a help to us. I'm not the greatest note-taker in the world."

"All right," said Charles, wondering how he could gracefully bring up the subject of a lawyer.

"Fine," said Lukowski, slapping a cassette into the machine. Before he pushed the record button, Charles asked him, "Aren't you supposed to read me my rights? You know, Miranda and all that."

Lukowski smiled. "No, you're not under arrest or anything."

"That comes later," said MacNab, eyes narrowing.

"Why don't you tell us about Dr. Bateman," began MacNab. "Back there in the shop you made it pretty clear you hated his guts, and that you were fooling around with his wife.''

''No, no, no,'' protested Charles. ''It's true, Dr. Bateman was difficult, and yes, I suppose I've said some heated things about him. But I wasn't fooling around with Mrs. Bateman.''

MacNab went over all this again, presumably for the tape recorder. Charles insisted that his relationship with Mrs. Bateman had consisted of his responding with some interest to her assault on him at a faculty party. He tried to act blasé about the fact that Dr. Bateman had jettisoned his career.

''Gee,'' said Lukowski, ''I guess he was a pretty terrible person to do that to you—not give you tenure and all.''

''I guess so,'' said Charles. ''I guess he was pretty terrible, but he's dead now and it doesn't seem to matter as much.''

''You mean you got it all off your chest, huh?'' said MacNab.

''No, that's not what I mean at all,'' said Charles.

''I guess he really pushed you to the wall,'' said Lukowski sympathetically. ''I mean, here you were, a respected professor, and now you're fixing cars. I mean it has to be kind of a comedown.''

''Not really,'' said Charles, wishing the fellow weren't so sympathetic.

''Well, it doesn't seem fair,'' said Lukowski.

''Life isn't fair,'' said Charles philosophically.

''I guess sometimes it seems tempting to try and make it fair,'' said Lukowski.

''Look,'' said Charles firmly, glancing at the tape recorder which hummed inexorably along, a strangely neutral fourth presence in the room, "I didn't like Dr. Bateman. Very few people did. But I didn't kill him. Period."

"Let's talk about where you were last Saturday," said MacNab.

"Saturday? Is that when, I mean did the doctor say . . ."

"Look, Charles," said MacNab. "We know that Bateman was last seen alive a week ago Saturday. He told people he was going to stop by and pick up a few groceries and that he was going to Cosmo's to complain about the lousy tune-up you people gave him." MacNab paused. "He's never been seen since."

"I wasn't even involved with Uncle Cosmo then," said Charles. "I hadn't been near the place in months. Uncle Cosmo didn't call me until later, after he'd won the lottery, to tell me he was handing over the business to me."

"But you knew the layout. Bud told us you knew about the spare key and where it was hidden," said MacNab.

"I guess so. But I had no reason to go down there."

"Unless you knew Bateman was going to be there," continued MacNab.

"I'd been avoiding Bateman," said Charles. "Ever since he'd told me about the tenure thing."

"So you had already learned about that," said Lukowski. "Gosh, it must have been a terrible blow."

"Well, yes. It was."

"When did you learn about it?" asked MacNab.

"The Friday before," said Charles.

MacNab nodded. "The day before, huh. And maybe Dr. Bateman mentioned that tune-up to you. His wife told us he'd complained about it to everyone. Seems logical he would have complained to you."

"His wife? You talked to her?"

"One of my associates did," said MacNab. "I'll be talking further to her later." He paused significantly. "I understand she's a very attractive woman—even in her grief."

"I suppose so," said Charles, trying to sound noncommittal. "Of course, she's older than I am. But attractive, well, yes."

"Apparently you thought so at that party," said MacNab. He pursued this angle for a while, and Charles twitched and explained that he had never met the woman before or after the faculty party.

"Kind of the older temptress type, I guess," said Lukowski, as if to imply that Charles would be putty in the hands of any old harridan who clapped eyes on him. "I guess it's natural she'd go after a good-looking young guy like you. Married to that obnoxious Bateman and all."

At this point it occurred to Charles he didn't have to respond to everything the detectives said, so he simply shut up. It took some effort, but on the whole, he thought it was more effective than trying to deny all the innuendos.

"We'll get into all that with other witnesses," said MacNab. "I'm sure the other people at the university, the people who were at that party and so forth, will have plenty to tell. Meanwhile, how about answering that last question. Where were you on the Saturday in question?"

Charles sighed. He'd been trying to stall. The answer was kind of embarrassing. Depressed over losing tenure, Charles had spent the whole weekend in his apartment. He'd read the papers, watched a bunch of movies on TV, consumed large amounts of junk food and beer, ceased shaving, and had generally gone to seed. The phone had rung a few times, but unwilling to discuss his disgrace with anyone, no matter how well meaning, he'd simply let it ring. He explained this to the detectives as gracefully as he could.

"You never left the apartment the whole weekend," said Lukowski. "Gee, that's too bad. Sounds kind of depressing too. You should have been out jogging or something. Would have been better for you."

"It was kind of depressing," said Charles lightly.

"Are you depressed a lot?" said Lukowski kindly.

"Oh, for heaven's sake," snapped Charles. "My career was ruined. I can't think of a better reason to be depressed. Naturally I was depressed. If a man can't go home and turn into a couch potato once in a while after getting a bad blow like that, well, when can he?"

"You were under a lot of stress," said Lukowski solemnly. "I can see that."

"What movies did you see on TV?" MacNab wanted to know.

Charles closed his eyes and ground his molars. He'd been afraid they'd ask that. "Well, one about the siege of Mafeking and the Boer War."

"Very educational, I'm sure," said MacNab. "Remember the title? Who was in it?"

"Poor Little Rich Girl. With Shirley Temple. Stanley Holloway had a song or two," Charles added helpfully.

"You were watching a Shirley Temple movie?" Lukowski seemed surprised. Charles imagined he'd shattered any illusions the detective may have had about college professors.

"That's right," said Charles defiantly. "And after that I watched *Tarzan Goes to India.* Tarzan tries to start an elephant sanctuary." He'd gone this far, he thought to himself, he may as well go all the way. "I don't know if it was Saturday or Sunday when I saw *Blondie Goes Latin*," he continued. "The whole weekend seemed to blur together."

MacNab gave him a heavy-lidded look. "I guess after all that brain work you'd been doing up at the university," he said with a sneer, "you needed to rest your mind."

CHAPTER
5

"I F we're all finished," said Charles, "I suppose I can go."

"Of course," said Lukowski. "You were making a voluntary statement in any case. Please, feel free to go home any time."

"Fine," said Charles, consulting his watch. "Although I'd really rather have you run me back to the shop so I can lock up."

The two detectives gave each other a look Charles couldn't interpret. Was he going to be arrested?

"Listen," growled MacNab, "we're not running a taxi service here. We're running a homicide investigation."

"You mean you took me downtown in a police car and I have to get back myself?"

"We're sorry for any inconvenience," said Lukowski. "But you understand, we do want to get on with our investigation. Do you have bus fare? Someone might be able to call you a cab."

"Oh, never mind," said Charles sulkily. He got up and left the room, sighing elaborately.

After he did, the two detectives leaned back in their chairs and seemed to relax.

MacNab and Lukowski had been partners for almost a year. MacNab was a third generation Seattle policeman. His twenty-odd years on the force had convinced him that there were very few causes of crime: sex, booze, drugs, greed, and plain old lunacy. He was powerfully built, direct, and irritable. Lukowski liked working with him because he had a lot of common sense. MacNab wore a heavy cologne, bits of gold jewelry, and loud sportscoats.

Lukowski was tall, thin, and rather striking with his prematurely gray hair, thick and silvery. He was in his early thirties. He'd started out as a treasury agent, but found the work too limiting. Treasury agents weren't in charge of enforcing very many laws. He'd been in Seattle ten years. His Chicago origins were evident in his flat vowels and his un-Western habit of wearing a wool topcoat in the winter, when everyone around him wore raincoats. A lapsed Catholic, Lukowski tended to see one or more of the seven deadly sins behind every crime he investigated.

"Well," said MacNab, "what do you think?"

"There's a good chance he's the guy," said Lukowski.

"He'll crack. He won't be able to take the pressure," said MacNab. "You just keep playing Mr. Nice Guy and I'll be the heavy, and some time soon I'll slip out for coffee and he'll crawl up into your lap sobbing and tell us all about it. Just be sure you Mirandize him right before he starts blabbing, and that it's on tape." He paused. "He'll get a good lawyer, get off on a psycho thing, how much you wanna bet?"

"You're moving kind of fast aren't you?" said Lukowski. "I mean we haven't even talked to the wife yet."

"I know, but Davis in missing persons told me she was pretty cut up about it on the phone last Saturday. He naturally assumed the old guy was just out screwing around or something, you know, it hadn't even been twenty-four hours when she got through to him, but she seemed distraught. Besides, it happened right in the guy's garage."

"Well, what about the uncle?" Lukowski fiddled with the cassette in the tape recorder and slipped it into his pocket.

"Believe me," said MacNab, "we've already seen our guy." He waved at the chair that Charles had been sitting in. "Motive and opportunity." He looked thoughtful. "Course it goes against my number one rule of homicide detection." He quoted the rule now. "Whenever you find a body, first of all ask yourself, is this body married?"

"Good rule," said Lukowski. "Let's check out the widow right away."

MacNab looked at his watch. "I could use a little overtime," he commented.

Mrs. Bateman received them eagerly. "I'm glad you're here," she said. "I can't believe it's happened, and I feel so helpless not knowing anything. It's been such a shock."

"Of course it has," said MacNab, his large frame drooping toward her with sympathy. Lukowski watched his partner with admiration. He always left the relatives to MacNab while he stood by and looked grave. MacNab expertly took the woman by the elbow and led her to one of her own chairs in the well-appointed living room. "We'll try not to take too much of your time. We just need to ask a few questions."

"Detective Davis from missing persons told me all about it," she said. "Finding him in that car. It's so horrible. I can't believe it."

MacNab murmured something soothing. Both men took in the surroundings quickly. A softly beige room with some good pictures and lots of books. A room that normally would have been tidy, but now showed signs of grief and distraction. A half-eaten meal on the coffee table next to an overflowing ashtray and a large tumbler that looked like it had brandy and melting ice cubes in it. Some needlepoint pillows on the floor.

Mrs. Bateman looked haggard. Her eyes were red rimmed and there were dark shadows beneath them. Her skin was ashen. But there was no denying she was a beautiful woman, probably in her late forties and well-preserved, with delicate, even features and big, dramatic blue eyes. The blond hair was a bleach job, but a good one, silvery and expensive looking. It was parted on the side and hung in one wave over the side of her face. She wore a black turtleneck sweater and a black tweed skirt.

"Where's Roland now?" she asked.

"We have to examine the body," said MacNab gently. "It should take a few days. Then it will be returned to you."

"I want to see him," she declared.

Lukowski thought of the huge wound in the skull and hoped the coroner could neaten things up a bit before that happened.

"The body's been identified," said MacNab, "by Dr. Carstairs."

"That young man in the department?" She looked confused.

"It was his garage," explained Lukowski.

"It was? Roland never told me that. He was always complaining about someone named Cosmo. What would Dr. Carstairs be doing at a car repair place?"

54

"It belonged to his uncle, Cosmo Sweeney," explained Lukowski. He watched carefully. She really seemed not to know about Carstairs's connection with the place. Now that she was told, would she suspect that Carstairs had killed her husband?

"How well did you know Charles Carstairs?" said Lukowski now.

"I'd just met him once," she said, gazing frankly into Lukowski's eyes. "I know he and Roland had had some problems."

"Do you think they were serious enough to cause Dr. Carstairs to want to harm your husband?" said MacNab.

She put her hand to her hair and shoved the big wave back from her face. "I don't think so. Anything is possible I suppose. Surely though, some stranger came in and did it. While Roland was waiting there."

Here it was, thought Lukowski. The convenient unkempt stranger, the homicidal maniac who just happened by.

"Waiting there?" he said. "At Cosmo's?"

"Yes. You see on Saturday Roland went out to do some errands. He was going to pick up a few things at the grocery store, and then, he said, he was going to that car place. Roland was quite agitated about a tune-up he got there. He said this Cosmo person wasn't giving him satisfaction, and he was going to get it, once and for all."

"Did he have an appointment?" said Lukowski.

"No. Cosmo had been evasive on the phone. Said he wasn't really open Saturdays, that he was in and out. But Roland was insistent. Roland told me he was going down there and waiting for Cosmo if he wasn't there, and he wasn't coming back until he'd had it out with him."

"I see," said MacNab.

Mrs. Bateman buried her face in her hands. "I feel so guilty," she said. "If I'd have gone with him maybe this wouldn't have happened."

"You mustn't blame yourself," said MacNab. "Who else knew Dr. Bateman would be at Cosmo's?"

She looked up. Lukowski was relieved to see she wasn't crying. "I don't know," she said. "He may have talked about his car problems to other members of the faculty."

"Did your husband have any enemies, Mrs. Bateman," said Lukowski.

"My husband was a wonderful man," she said. "Everyone loved and admired him. Why just Saturday night he was to be honored by the board of the Columbia Museum. They were giving him a special plaque and everything. The mayor was going to be there." Her eyes filled with tears now. "That's when I knew, when he didn't come home in time to dress for that dinner. It was to be a lovely affair. Black tie, very elegant. He would never miss that. So when he didn't come back in time I called the police."

Lukowski braced himself for a tirade against the police. He knew how angry relatives of victims always were about the twenty-four-hour rule. They always claimed their relatives would be alive today if missing persons had swung into action immediately. Mrs. Bateman didn't complain, though. She just sobbed a little and reached out for the watery brandy, took a sip, and seemed to pull herself together.

"Mrs. Bateman," said MacNab, "is there someone who can stay with you for a while?"

"Oh, the dear dean and his wife have asked me if I want to stay with them. The dean and Roland were boyhood friends. But I just want to be alone for a while."

"Of course," said MacNab. "We'll be in touch with

you." He handed her his card. "Call me if anything comes up." He rose to leave, and Lukowski followed suit. "There's just one thing," said MacNab offhandedly, "I'd like to know. Is there any reason why your husband might have been jealous of Dr. Carstairs?"

Her eyes widened. "You mean academically? Of course not."

"There was never any, um, flirtation, between you and . . ."

"I was devoted to Roland Bateman," said Mrs. Bateman, placing her hand on her bosom dramatically. "I did meet the young man once, and we got along well. Roland may have misinterp—"

She stopped.

"You're a very attractive woman, Mrs. Bateman," said Lukowski in businesslike tones.

Mrs. Bateman looked at him, a pleased smile beginning to form on her tired face.

"I suppose I am," she said complacently. "And one of the prices a woman pays for good looks is spiteful gossip. If anyone suggests I was anything other than a devoted wife to Roland, they are simply lying."

"We have to ask a lot of questions, Mrs. Bateman," said MacNab. "Because nothing is more important than finding out who killed your husband. I'm sure you'll agree."

She nodded.

"Where were you on Saturday the twelfth?" said MacNab.

"Here at home. Waiting for him. Wondering where he was."

Lukowski gazed over at the mantelpiece. A large and handsome Chinese vase stood at one end of it next to a brass candlestick. On the other end of the mantel stood just a single brass candlestick. The arrangement was so obviously asymmetrical that Lukowski stared at it for a moment.

Mrs. Bateman followed his gaze and promptly burst into tears. "Roland loved beautiful things," she said. "He loved that pair of vases. On Saturday, while he was gone, the cat got up there and knocked it off. Roland would have died if he'd known," she continued, unconscious of irony. Openly sobbing now, she said, "I wonder if it happened just as . . . Oh, it's too horrible."

Lukowski had hoped that Mrs. Bateman wouldn't fall apart while they were there; a cowardly feeling, he knew.

"You've had a terrible shock," said MacNab. "Perhaps a doctor could give you—"

Mrs. Bateman waved her hand impatiently. "I've got plenty of Valium," she said. She turned back to the mantel. "There were two, and now there's only one," she said, and in case they didn't get the point, she said, "just like me and Roland."

The two men took their leave, insisting she not show them out. As they closed the door behind them, Lukowski happened to look down at his feet. There, embedded in the fibers of the welcome mat, was a shard of porcelain from the twin of the Chinese vase he'd been sorry he'd noticed. Thinking that finding it there might disturb Mrs. Bateman, he picked it up and threw it into a dense mass of shrubbery.

CHAPTER

6

THERE were several reasons Charles decided to go to Dr. Bateman's funeral.

First of all, Detective MacNab had made it clear he thought Charles was a suspect. And on TV and in the movies, the police were always on hand at the funeral of the victim, lurking ominously in the back of the church, cold eyes flitting over the faces of the mourners. Charles felt if he showed up and looked suitably respectful, he might seem less guilty.

Secondly, Charles was still in shock, amazed that someone had actually done it, killed Dr. Bateman. He wanted to know who it had been. Maybe, as in all those TV shows and movies, the murderer would be on hand. Charles planned to check out the crowd. He wasn't sure just what to look for. Guilt and remorse? Fear of discovery, revealed by nervous twitching? A grim smile of satisfaction?

Finally, Charles decided to go to the funeral because of last night's phone call from JoAnne, one of the department secretaries. Everyone in the department joked about the crush she had on Charles. Charles couldn't quite see it, although she was always extremely helpful in a kind of pink and breathy way, staying late to type for him and so forth. And she'd made it a point to tell him how sorry she was about this tenure business. In fact, she was the only one who'd said much of anything. Mostly, his colleagues ducked when they saw him coming, and if he succeeded in making eye contact they acted uncomfortable.

JoAnne had told him about the funeral and about the reception that was to follow at the dean's house. All faculty were invited, and she was calling in her official capacity. "By the way," she added, "I thought you should know there's been some talk around the department. About you and Dr. Bateman."

Could they think he'd killed Dr. Bateman? Next to not getting tenure, Charles thought that being suspected of killing your department chairman had to be the very worst possible thing, careerwise. He tried to frame some reply to the unspoken allegation, but JoAnne went on. "They think that with him out of the picture, well, you know, passed away, that maybe you could get tenure. Everyone knows he had it in for you."

"I see," said Charles thoughtfully. He immediately decided to go to that funeral and that reception at the dean's house. He could test the waters and maybe do a little gentle lobbying. Nothing overt, of course, considering the solemnity of the occasion.

"If you want to go," said JoAnne, "maybe we could go together." Charles was silent. "I mean, I thought you might feel more comfortable *with* someone. Considering this tenure thing and all."

"That's nice of you JoAnne, but I don't know just what my plans are."

"All right." She sounded a little disappointed.

Charles wasn't going to show up leaning on one of the secretaries. He meant to exude a scholarly dignity, and let them all see he wasn't going to be petty and boycott the funeral just because Bateman had wrecked his career.

The service was held in a fashionable Episcopal church near Lake Washington. All in all, Charles thought, Bateman would have liked it. A doleful rendition of "Gaudeamus Igitur," which Charles recognized from his high school production of *The Student Prince*, a traditional liturgy, some Victorian hymns of a martial nature, a tasteful black coffin with touches of brass, a simple white wreath.

The dean, a boyhood friend of Dr. Bateman, delivered a eulogy, touching on amusing anecdotes from Dr. Bateman's childhood, and the grown Bateman's purported encouragement of youth and devotion to scholarship. There was nothing trendy at this funeral—no attempt at whimsy or at making a lot of atheists and agnostics feel comfortable in church, like a Unitarian funeral Charles had attended that featured balloons and banjo music.

Craning around during the final hymn, Charles spotted Detectives MacNab and Lukowski, just as in the movies, staring out at the assembled company. Charles caught their eye, then turned around, looking slightly embarrassed.

This distraction aside, Charles found the service oddly moving. Sure, Bateman had been a first class son-of-a-bitch, but lying there in his coffin (Charles imagined the corpse wearing academic robes), the professor didn't seem so formidable. After all, he was dead, so he was mortal and human. For the first time, it dawned on Charles that whoever had bashed in Dr. Bateman's skull shouldn't have.

Driving up to the dean's house, Charles felt a pang at

his ruined career. The house was in an expensive neighborhood. It was a big brick Tudor thing with a large, well-kept garden, and it exuded prosperity and security. True, faculty of Charles's generation could never aspire to such luxury in today's real estate market. Charles had heard the dean had picked this place up for a song during the Boeing slump of the sixties, when Seattle houses were cheap.

The dean's wife, who never remembered anyone, and was famous for treating visiting junior faculty like a lot of unruly children whom she was forced to entertain once in a while, answered the door and directed him perfunctorily to the living room. It had a big window with a view of the lake, a large Oriental carpet, and some overstuffed velvet furniture. A long buffet table was set up by the window.

As soon as he arrived, Charles spotted the widow and felt it his painful duty to speak to her. She wore a modest black dress and looked pale. He gave her his hand and said, "I'm so sorry." He wouldn't have recognized her as the vivacious blond of the faculty party. She looked smaller and older, although Mrs. Bateman was one of those women who could be anything between thirty-five and fifty. Charles had once heard the department secretaries discussing her age and speculating that she'd had a facelift. "Check out her neck," one of them said. "They can't do that much with necks."

"The police have made horrible insinuations about us," she said dramatically. Charles winced. "Of course I told them there was nothing between us."

"Of course," said Charles.

"I'm glad you came," she said. "Roland really *did* like you."

What could he say to this? He came up with "I hope so."

"Perhaps we could have lunch sometime," she continued. "I'm sure Roland would want me to get out and see people." Charles doubted any such thing, judging by Bateman's reaction in the kitchen that night. "This must be a very difficult time for you," he murmured, wondering how to get her to let go of his hand.

"Roland was a fine man, don't you agree?" she said.

What else could Charles do under the circumstances. "A fine man," he repeated.

"So sensitive and caring. We had a wonderful life together."

"That must have been very gratifying."

"Tell me exactly what you thought about him," persisted Mrs. Bateman. "It helps me to hear from others what an extraordinary man he really was."

Charles took a deep breath and racked his brain for a reply. "Dr. Bateman," he said, "made a deep impression on me. Everything my career is today, I owe to him. I shall never forget him."

Mrs. Bateman smiled a sad, Garboesque smile, and he pulled his hand away. He wondered if he could get a drink here. And soon.

A quick glance around the room told him that all eyes had been on him and Mrs. Bateman as they had talked. Her strange look of intensity, which he'd found so charming at the faculty party, doubtless gave everyone the wrong impression. Everyone probably wondered if the torrid affair he was supposed to have been having with her was still going on, or if the two of them would wait to resume their activities until Dr. Bateman was a little colder in his grave.

At one end of the buffet table was the department's pro-Bateman faction, led by Dr. Smathers. They looked solemn as they picked over crab legs, asparagus wrapped in thinly sliced ham, rolls, and roast beef. At the other end of the table was the department's anti-Bateman faction, a younger group. They eyed the first group edgily and sipped wine from plastic glasses.

Charles had always tried to walk a fine line between the two groups. Until his own troubles with the chairman had begun, the system had worked well. Now, Charles didn't know quite what to do. It was clear, though, that if he was to get himself back into the department he'd have to ingratiate himself with everyone he could. Who knew where the balance of power now lay?

He went over and got himself some wine, smiling a little nervously at everyone. He hoped that the shock of Dr. Bateman's death would erase from their minds his embarrassing failure to get tenure.

"Consoling the grieving widow, eh? How's she holding up?" Charles's office mate, Bill Gunderson, had approached, with a plate of something in his hand. Bill had been distant with Charles after the ax fell, but now presumably, with Dr. Bateman stone-cold dead, Bill had less to risk. Charles had always thought that underneath a casual, gossipy exterior, Bill Gunderson was a sneaky, conniving manipulator and Machiavellian master of departmental politics, but Charles needed friends now, so he gave him a big smile and acted pleased to see him.

"I really don't know," said Charles. "I barely know the woman."

"Sure," said Bill, with a knowing look. "Well if that's your story I advise you to stick with it."

"It's true," said Charles feebly.

"Skip it. Had any of the food? Pretty good, but word is it's all left over from a party the humanities division had for the Board of Regents last week. I wouldn't risk the aioli sauce. Or the crab legs." He popped a tiny sandwich into his mouth. "So where've you been? No one's seen you around much."

Charles shrugged. "I've just been showing up to teach my classes. To tell you the truth, Bill, I haven't had the heart to do much more, after my big disappointment."

"Yeah. That was a tough break. I imagine you're wondering if with Bateman gone you might appeal and get back in."

"Not really," lied Charles. "I'll be sending out resumés, and I've been looking at some opportunities in the private sector."

"Working for your uncle again, huh?" said Gunderson, looking down meaningfully at Charles's hands. It was impossible to ever get the grease completely out from beneath the fingernails, even for a state occasion like Dr. Bateman's wake.

"Of course I wouldn't be opposed to any movement, that is, if there's any sympathy in the department that could be channeled—"

Bill cut him off. "If you want anything like that you're going to have to initiate it yourself. And I guess you heard who's acting chairman."

"Not really," said Charles, feeling ashamed at his ignorance. It made him feel even more of an outsider.

"Smathers."

"Oh." This was grim news indeed. Smathers was Bateman's protégé. He'd spent years toadying up to the old boy.

"My God," said Bill, obviously startled. "Look who's here. I guess they gave him a three-day pass for the funeral."

Charles turned to look at the arched entry to the room. There stood Larry de la Roque, a legend in the department. Larry was about Charles's age and had been working, for as long as anyone could remember, on his doctoral dissertation. Dr. Bateman had been his advisor.

The dissertation, something about violence and how it wasn't really aberrational when viewed from the proper perspective, was always supposed to be in its final stages.

"What do you mean?" said Charles.

"You *have* been out of the picture," said Bill. "Larry finally thinks he's got it all pulled together, the damn thing's at the typist and everything, and then, zap, out of the blue Bateman didn't approve his request to extend the standard ten-year deadline."

"Wow," said Charles.

"Yeah. So Larry had a breakdown. They actually carted him away. He committed himself voluntarily, so I guess he let himself out again."

"Larry has been a regular fixture in the department for years," said Charles.

"I know. And Bateman had him teaching huge classes for a third of what a regular professor would get. I guess he figured if Larry finally did get his Ph.D. he'd cost too much for what he could deliver."

"What a shame," said Charles, sympathetic, although he'd never liked Larry and found his dissertation topic vaguely disturbing.

"I notice he's wearing that same corduroy suit," continued Bill. "I think he arrived in that ten years ago, and he's worn it ever since. Pathetic, isn't it?"

Larry de la Roque did look pathetic in his worn brown corduroy suit, his long, lanky hair now streaked with gray. Charles congratulated himself on having borrowed a good-looking dark blue suit from his brother-in-law to wear to the funeral. At least he didn't *look* like Larry, even though he felt a new kinship with the man. After all, what was so different about the years they'd toiled away in the department if the results were the same? Tossed out on their ears, at a mere caprice of Roland Bateman.

"I wonder if he did it," mused Bill.

"Did what?" Charles brought himself back from the depressing thoughts of his own similarity to Larry.

"You know. Killed Bateman. It's been done before. That horrible case at Stanford. The guy killed his advisor. He'd been working on his dissertation for a little longer, though." Gunderson looked thoughtful. "It might be interesting to study perennial Ph.D. candidates. Figure when they snap. And what organizational factors push them over the edge."

"Maybe he did," said Charles, looking over at Larry in awe.

"Well *somebody* did," said Bill. "Maybe it was Larry. Or you. Or the widow." He gestured over at Mrs. Bateman, who was leaning on the arm of the dean and greeting new arrivals. "Or maybe Smathers. Word is Bateman was about to publish some of Smathers's research as his own."

"How could he do that?" Charles asked, aghast.

Bill shrugged. "Who knows? Maybe Bateman had something on him."

"Like what?" Charles looked over at Dr. Smathers, a weasely little man with thick glasses.

"Plagiarism," said Bill in a funny definite way. "Just a rumor," he added hastily, fending off further questioning. "Of course I guess the best suspect is still you. After all, it happened at your uncle's garage, didn't it?"

"Come on, Bill, you don't think I—"

"Of course not. And when the police come to question us all that's just what I'll tell them. Everyone is getting interviewed later. But I guess they already talked to you."

"Good," said Charles. "Maybe they can pursue some leads here. After all, Bateman had plenty of enemies in the department. It's bound to come out."

"Oh, I wouldn't count on that," said Bill. "You know how it is. The department just closes ranks. Don't want to air any of that dirty linen. Might have to testify about it later, for God's sake. Besides, I bet the cops won't be interested in these academic problems. A juicy triangle. Raw sex. That's more up their alley." He gazed significantly in the direction of the widow.

Bill Gunderson was beginning to remind Charles more and more of a junior Dr. Bateman. He seemed to take sadistic pleasure in stacking the case against Charles.

Suddenly, Charles wanted to be out of this house and away from his soon-to-be ex-colleagues. The prospect of an afternoon listening to Steve snarl, wondering what was the matter with Phil, and trying to get Bud to put in an honest day's work seemed almost soothing.

But before Charles went back to the shop he thought he'd better do a little more sleuthing. After all, the sooner Dr. Bateman's killer was found, the sooner life would be back to normal. Charles even briefly fantasized that with the real killer unmasked, the faculty would rally around Charles, feel sorry he was ever suspected, and give him tenure.

Gingerly he went closer to the buffet table and approached Larry de la Roque. "Hi," he said, aware that speaking to him now might seem odd after a decade of avoiding him. De la Roque had always had the unfortunate habit of discussing his unfinished dissertation with anyone who would listen.

"Hello," said Larry blandly. "I guess you're here for the same reason I am."

"What's that?" Charles hoped his desire to worm his way back into the good graces of the department wasn't so transparent. Although perhaps Larry was referring to the food. Larry was notorious for scarfing up any free food and drink that came his way.

"To see if the old bastard was really dead."

Charles gave Larry a nervous smile. Maybe he was completely insane. Maybe he'd start going berserk right here at the dean's house. Charles imagined a scene with Larry throwing crab legs around and screaming, culminating in an emotional confession. It seemed people used to do that on the old Perry Mason show all the time. "Yes, I did it, and I'm glad," they would say from the back of the courtroom.

Larry looked calm enough now, although he was probably sedated. He began to pile food on his plate, as was his usual custom. It was presumably because he was a starving grad student. Hunger had been a good incentive for Charles to get his own dissertation finished.

"The food is great," said Charles mildly, as Larry scooped up a handful of tiny sandwiches.

"Yes, better than the food I've been getting. Nothing but starch."

"Oh?"

"I guess you heard. I checked myself into the state hospital."

"Well, yes, I had heard something about that," said Charles, trying to make a stint in the state loony bin sound like a respectable academic retreat.

Larry, stuffing the sandwiches in his mouth, turned and stared intently at Charles. "But I'm not crazy."

"No, of course not."

"I just had to let them think that. Or I would have been facing assault charges."

"Oh?"

"I guess you heard I took it kind of hard when Bateman didn't extend my deadline." Larry spoke with his mouth full. Charles watched crumbs fall to the corduroy lapels, followed by spurts of paté.

"What did you do, exactly?"

Larry narrowed his eyes. "I trashed his office. Pulled over a few file cabinets. Then I threw his in-basket at him." He looked entirely unremorseful. "Then I went for his throat."

"I guess you weren't yourself," said Charles.

"No, I was finally myself. I realized, when I saw that pompous smirk on his face, that the man was a monster. He was also a poor scholar, and unfit to make judgments on me. And here I was, under his thumb. 'I like you, de la Roque,' that's what he said to me. Right before he told me I couldn't have more time."

"Yeah. He said the same thing to me before he told me he'd screwed up tenure for me."

"Anyway, it was neat throwing things at him. He was really scared. I decided then and there that my dissertation was perfect. As you may recall, I've been collecting a lot of data that proves that a certain level of violence is indicative of a healthy society. I've changed the title again, I guess you didn't know that. Now it's called 'Homicide as a Means of Utility Maximization by a Rational Actor When Confronted by a Nonlegitimated Authoritarian Structure.'" Larry chomped some more while this sunk in, then continued, "I always knew it was a superb piece of scholarship, but it wasn't until I terrorized Bateman that I knew how liberating and exciting violence can be on a personal level.'' Larry guzzled some Chablis. ''I won't have any trouble finishing that dissertation now,'' he concluded.

''I thought your deadline—'' began Charles.

''Nope. Bateman died before he finished the paperwork. I'm starting my application for extension all over again. With Smathers.''

''Maybe he'll give it to you,'' said Charles dubiously.

''He'd better,'' said Larry confidently.

''Well,'' said Charles nervously, sidling away, ''take it easy.''

''Take it easy?'' Larry practically shouted. ''Why should I? Nature red in tooth and claw, that's my world view from now on, Charles.'' And, as if to illustrate the point, he seized a large crab claw and began noisily sucking the pink flesh out of it.

A thought occurred to Charles. ''By the way,'' he said mildly, ''when did you get out, er, leave the, you know, hospital.''

''Yesterday,'' said Larry triumphantly. ''And the bastard was alive and kicking when they pulled me off of him ten days ago. Too bad. I would have been proud to have taken him out.''

Suddenly Larry put his arm around Charles in a confidential manner. ''You know what?'' he stage whispered. ''If you did it, I salute you. More power to you.''

Charles extricated himself from Larry's embrace and left him to his pillaging of the buffet. Beside the discomfort of finding himself in the clutches of a lunatic, Charles wanted to avoid food stains on his borrowed clothes. It would be a nuisance to have to take his brother-in-law's suit to the cleaners before he returned it.

Fortifying himself with another glass of Chablis and

some paté, Charles decided he'd better tackle Smathers before he left. After all, Smathers was now apparently the man to deal with in the department.

Smathers was looking morosely into his own wineglass, and when he looked up in response to Charles's greeting, Charles thought he saw him flinch.

"Oh, hello, Carstairs," he said, casting his eyes around the room for someone else to talk to. "Didn't expect to see you here."

"Well, I am still part of the department," Charles said optimistically. "I understand you'll be taking over for poor Bateman."

"Yes, and I hope to carry on Dr. Bateman's fine work." Smathers blinked behind the thick glasses. Charles reflected that now Bateman was gone, Smathers was the last person in the department to use the title *doctor* and to expect to be addressed that way himself. "I noticed you talking to Larry de la Roque," he said with a little frown.

Charles wanted to disassociate himself completely from a disgruntled failure and to ingratiate himself with Dr. Smathers, so he said, "Yes. We talked. To be quite candid I'm a little worried about him."

"Why? He'll be all right. He wasn't suited for academic life in the first place."

"No, not that. I don't mean worried about *him*. I mean, he sounded a little, well, volatile."

"The man's insane," said Smathers. "The commitment laws in this state are a scandal. He should be locked up." Then, as if regretting this outburst, he added nervously, "That is, I'm not a psychiatrist, but I think . . ."

"He tells me he expects you to extend his deadline," said Charles, enjoying the flicker of fear that followed this revelation. Smathers was a notorious gutless wonder and hated all unpleasantness.

72

"Well, he can't see me. It's that simple," said Smathers. "You're his friend. You tell him that. I won't let him past the secretaries. *They'll* have to deal with him. That's what they get paid for." His hand was trembling.

"He's not *my* friend," said Charles.

"It's very simple. My policy is to continue as if Dr. Bateman were alive. I see no point in dredging up old controversies and rehashing them. What's been decided is decided."

"I see," said Charles.

"Yes, I thought you would. You understand, don't you? Gunderson was over here telling me you might want to appeal that tenure decision. If I let you have tenure then de la Roque will wonder why I won't extend his deadline. I mean, I have to be fair."

"I hadn't thought of it that way," said Charles, his teeth beginning to grind for the first time since he'd arrived. "But it's not as though I threw an in-basket at anyone, is it?"

"Heavens no. I never suggested you killed Dr. Bateman," said Smathers somewhat hysterically. "Now if you'll excuse me I must talk to the dean." He set his glass down and went away.

Charles sighed. His subtle lobbying hadn't worked out so well. His sleuthing wasn't much better. Larry appeared to have a solid alibi. And Charles hadn't even managed to get on the subject of plagiarism and stolen research with Smathers, following up on Bill Gunderson's lead. Smathers seemed to suspect Charles. He was actually afraid of him. Well, that could only prove he was innocent himself. Mrs. Bateman, another suspect, seemed genuinely sorrowful at her husband's death.

Surely Dr. Bateman had more enemies. He looked around

the room and noticed another professor, Eleanor Zimmer. Eleanor had certainly hated Bateman. A rather fierce-looking woman with heavy eyebrows and wild, dark hair, Eleanor had filed sex discrimination complaints against Bateman after he circulated a memo, obviously aimed at her, about breast-feeding during office hours.

Charles didn't suspect her, but felt like talking to someone reasonably friendly before he left. He waved and she came over. Usually in baggy jeans and sweaters, Eleanor looked strange in a prim dark dress.

"Plastic glasses," she hissed "Wonder what she's saving the crystal for?" Eleanor gestured to china cabinets full of wineglasses. "Say, listen Charles, I'm real sorry about the tenure thing. It was a bad deal, no question. I guess I should have spoken up, but I was exhausted from my own battles with the department." She left unspoken the thought that Charles hadn't exactly rallied to her defense when Bateman had been circulating that memo about "female employees and exposed secondary sex characteristics."

"There's nothing you could have done," he said. "I guess I'm starting life as a mechanic now. I've been managing my uncle's garage."

"Good for you," said Eleanor. "A real job. You'll probably make a lot of money. I wish I could get out of the department. Pigs, most of them. I guess you know who's in charge now?"

"Yeah, Smathers." Charles sighed. "I was just talking to him."

"Smathers," she snorted. "That pusillanimous wimp." Charles was a little uneasy. Eleanor sorted men into two categories: pigs and wimps. He wondered where he fit in.

"I wish I had a garage to manage," said Eleanor.

Charles was tempted to hand the business over to her right then and there. "But I'm working on my own escape plan. You know that research I did on women's roles in West Coast Indian tribes? I'm turning it into a big trashy novel. A bodice ripper. About a white girl raised by Indians who becomes a famous warrior. And then she meets a Spanish don or a sea captain or something."

"Well, good luck, Eleanor," said Charles, somewhat taken aback. She was one of the department's best scholars, and as he recalled, her research into women's roles among West Coast Indians hadn't turned up anything like women warriors. "I don't know why you don't like academic life, though. I'd be happy to get back into it."

"There's got to be something better in life for a nice guy like you," she said. Charles thought that *nice guy* meant she put him in the wimp category. He realized he'd rather have been a pig. "There's got to be something more worthwhile than fighting these jerks here all your life," she continued. "As you know, it's enough to drive someone to murder." She looked taken aback. "Oh, I'm sorry, Charles. I didn't mean that. I don't care what they all say. *I* don't think you killed him."

From across the room, Charles heard a thud and raised voices in concerned tones. Mrs. Bateman, it appeared, had fainted. She was being propped up now, and the dean's wife was administering brandy.

CHAPTER
7

I T seemed as good a time as any to leave.

Where everyone gathered around the fallen Mrs. Bateman, Charles hovered on the edge of the circle, draining the last of his cheap Chablis. If he left now, he thought, he wouldn't have to say good-bye to anyone, and could slink out unobserved. Remembering he wouldn't have time for lunch, he crammed a few more tiny sandwiches into his mouth, á la Larry de la Roque.

He'd made it to the front door, when he heard Mrs. Bateman's voice: "I'm sorry. It's been such a shock. But I'm so glad Roland had so many *dear* friends." Murmurs of relief came from her audience. He knew he should feel sorry for Mrs. Bateman, but her theatrical manner made it difficult. Maybe her dramatic gestures and phrases were a reflection of honest emotions. Charles suspected, however, that instead they covered a large, vacant space. In some ways, the Batemans had been meant for each other.

Outside the house, with its oppressive atmosphere, the air was cool and the garden was wet and shiny. As it often does in Seattle in the spring, it rained gently. Charles, a Seattle native, never minded much. He found something vaguely comforting in the sight of sky muffled by gray clouds. He liked the sensation of driving to the accompaniment of clacking windshield wipers, tires hissing along wet asphalt.

Instead of going home to change, Charles felt an overwhelming desire to stop by the shop and see how things were going. In the three days since Dr. Bateman's body had been discovered, business had been terrible. The police had taken away a lot of tools, the press had been all over, and appointments had had to be rescheduled. Some customers didn't want to reschedule. They just cancelled.

Today, however, there were six jobs booked, and it could be profitable *if* the work got out. Charles was tormented by the vision of the mechanics lolling around at his expense while irate customers brooded in the waiting area. He wanted to get back there and check it out.

He also hoped Sylvia Snow would have something concrete to tell him about the financial picture. She was sitting at a tall stool at the front counter when he came in. Today she was wearing a gaudy Mexican peasant dress over orange tights and turtleneck. Peculiar flat canvas shoes completed her costume.

"How are you coming along?" he asked her, wondering anew if someone who looked like a waitress at a macrobiotic restaurant would be able to solve his bookkeeping problems. He gave a little frown.

"I'm sorry it seems to be taking so long," she said. "But the records are in terrible order."

Charles sighed and went into the back. Steve was working energetically under the one lift in the shop, tightening bolts with the air compressor. Charles noticed Steve always had use of the better equipment. Probably terrorized the other guys away from it.

Phil, leaning under an open hood, was looking puzzled as he examined an engine, and Bud was actually doing something of an automotive nature as well. His short legs appeared from beneath a Volkswagen van.

"Hi, guys," said Charles, trying to contain the nervousness the whole state of the operation gave him. "Everything okay?"

"No, it's not," snapped Steve. "This is a '73 I'm working on. The parts that arrived this morning were for a '74. That broad you hired said she'd take care of it. Not that she knows anything about cars."

"Relax," said Charles. "Everything will smooth out soon."

"I *told* you I want all my parts ready when the fucking job starts," said Steve, walking over to the lift controls and banging at the mechanism to let the car down.

For the first time he turned to Charles and looked at him. "Say, you're all dressed up. You look like a fucking banker."

"I was at a funeral," explained Charles.

"Yeah? Well how you gonna run this place right if you're off at a funeral? You want this place to run right you gotta stay on top of things."

Charles ignored him and walked over to where Phil was puzzling over an engine. Phil nodded a greeting. "I guess it's that battery," he mused. Charles started to ask more about it, preparatory to venturing an opinion, when he remembered Phil was an expert on wiring and charging problems.

"I'm sure you'll figure it out," he said in a reassuring manner.

"Well take a look at this," said Phil, beckoning him over. "Watch what happens when I turn it on."

Charles peered into the engine compartment while Phil went behind the wheel and started the car. Making a mental note not to get grease on the suit he'd successfully defended from Larry de la Roque, Charles gave himself some distance. But when the engine started, oil came gushing out of the engine compartment like a miniature oil well, splattering Charles's jacket and leaving a trail of dark spots on the trousers too.

"Gee, I'm sorry," said Phil. "I forgot I pulled the oil filter. I'm really sorry. There's so much wrong with this car I didn't know which system to check first."

Charles looked down at his suit. The fabric seemed to be sucking oil deep into its fibers. Phil began to mop away at Charles with a shop towel, apologizing pitifully the whole time.

"It's all right," said Charles between clenched teeth, as he fended off the mopping operation.

"I feel so bad," said Phil.

"It's all right. It's my fault for having worn this suit into the shop."

"I can't believe I forgot I pulled that filter," said Phil, his face crumpling with sorrow.

Charles was reminded of Thomas Carlyle, who ended up comforting John Stuart Mill because Mill felt so terrible about having inadvertently destroyed Carlyle's manuscript. He also wondered just how high-strung Phil was, and whether something like this would send him off the deep end. There were six cars to get out today.

Charles looked over at the Volkswagen van and noticed that Bud's legs emerging from beneath it were still in the same position. He leaned over and said in a kindly way, "What's the matter? You got a tough bolt under there that won't move? Want some Liquid Wrench to loosen it up?"

There was no answer. With a horrible feeling in his gut, Charles imagined that Bud lay dead under the car. This was all he needed. Another body. He seized a trouble light hanging nearby and switched it on, shining it under the car.

Bud lay there, his head tipped back, his eyes closed, his mouth slightly open. He was snoring. Charles gave the soles of Bud's greasy work Wellingtons a sharp kick. Bud blinked and roused himself, lifting up his head and banging it on the undercarriage of the van. "Oof," he said.

"Everything okay under there?" said Charles. "Comfortable?"

"Gee, I must have dropped off," said Bud. He began slowly wrenching.

Terrific, thought Charles as he picked his way through cars and tools back to the office. A narcoleptic, probably. There had to be better help available. More motivated than Bud, more civil than Steve, more mentally stable than Phil.

"Hey, the professor got grease all over himself," said Steve cheerily as Charles walked past him.

"Shut up and fix cars," snapped Charles.

"I'm going to run home and change, and then stop by the dry cleaner's and come right back," he said to Sylvia Snow. "You don't mind catching the phones some more, do you?"

"No, not at all." She gazed at him. "What a mess. You should have put a coverall on over your suit before you went back there."

"I know that," said Charles irritably.

"There were a few messages this morning," said Sylvia, handing him some small squares of paper. "These people claim you screwed up their transmission." Charles vaguely remembered a few previous calls on the same theme. "They say they're coming down here in person to get satisfaction." It sounded as if he were being challenged to a duel. "And Detective MacNab called just a minute ago, while you were back there. He said he's coming over and he wants you to stay here until he gets here."

Charles sighed. "Oh, all right. I suppose I can find something useful to do for a few minutes while I wait."

"Yes, you can," she replied in a school-mistressy tone Charles found irritating. She waved a file folder at him. "These are receivables. People who never paid your uncle. It comes to about three thousand dollars. Right now, outside of that tow truck outside, it looks like your biggest asset, so I suggest you get on the phone and tell these people to pay up."

Charles looked shocked. "You mean ask people for *money?*"

"That's right. *Your* money. I don't know why he extended credit. One of the best things you have going for you in this business is that you can collect as soon as the work is done."

"I'm sure Uncle Cosmo was just being compassionate. These people probably needed their cars."

"If they couldn't afford to have their cars fixed, they should have taken the bus. I've done that myself."

Charles tried to remember, back in his student days, about the phone calls he used to get about his stereo payments. A firm tone, he recalled, with a hint of menace. "Couldn't you do it?" he said, smiling nicely.

She curled her lip. "If you want this business to work, you'll have to get tougher."

He grabbed the file. "Oh, all right." The folder, labeled in Uncle Cosmo's familiar block capitals *Deadbeats*, had copies of the unpaid invoices with the customers' names, addresses, and phone numbers.

He tried the first one. A high, nasal voice of indeterminate sex came on. He was relieved to hear it was an answering machine. Good. He wouldn't have to talk to them directly. "If you have a message for Bob or Madge, or for the Pacific Institute of Holistic Hypnotherapy, or for Adopt-A-Seal, Inc., or for the Little Nell Day Care Center, please leave it at the sound of the tone."

Bob and Madge certainly sounded enterprising. Too bad that despite all their endeavors they still couldn't pay their bills. Charles spoke up at the tone. "Hi, this is Cosmo's Car Center. We'd sure appreciate hearing from you about your past-due bill. Give us a call." That hadn't been too hard.

"They had a machine," he explained to Sylvia, who had been watching and listening the whole time.

"Never say it's about a bill to a machine," she said. "They'll never call back."

Charles suspected this was true, and went on to the next number. A Mrs. Lindstrom admitted she owed Cosmo's one hundred and five dollars. "But I've just had an operation," she explained in a weak voice. "They took a stone out of me as big as a grapefruit."

"I'm sorry to hear that," said Charles sympathetically, but after glancing at Miss Snow's disapproving face he added hastily, "But we do need payment on this invoice. Could you give us something on account?"

"My health has always been poor," continued Mrs. Lindstrom. "Looks I'll be going under the knife again soon. Female troubles. They've got to take out—"

Charles cut her off. "Send us a little something soon," he said, and ended the conversation.

Sylvia looked disappointed. "Try and get a commitment for a specific amount on a specific date," she said. "Leaving it open-ended like that makes it too easy for them to do nothing."

"I'm sure you're right," said Charles. "But please bear with me. I've had a trying morning. I just got grease all over my brother-in-law's best suit. Before that I went to a horrible reception where I learned my career is probably incapable of resuscitation. I was insulted by colleagues, and I probably ate tainted food. Before that I had to sit on a hard pew and listen to a pompous eulogy for a guy I hated. I had to try and act sorry that he was dead in front of a lot of people and—"

The expression on Sylvia Snow's face looked so strange that Charles stopped speaking. It was frozen in a pale mask, but the big dark eyes were widened and rolling to one side. Maybe she was going to have some kind of fit. The place was turning into a neurological nightmare, what with the narcoleptic Bud and Phil's unnamed psychotic problems. Steve, with his outbursts of profanity, was probably suffering from Tourette's Syndrome.

Just then MacNab's voice spoke up. "Go on. What was it you were saying? How much you hated Dr. Bateman?"

Charles realized Miss Snow's peculiar expression had been meant to warn him that the police had just come in.

MacNab stood there grinning, and next to him stood Lukowski with his shy smile.

"We've been all over that," snapped Charles. "Do we have to go through it all again?"

MacNab twirled a heavy diamond ring on his little finger. "Just want to go over a few things. Make sure we got everything straight."

"Hey, you got grease all over that nice suit," said Lukowski kindly. " What a shame."

"Professional hazard," said Charles airily.

"You should wear coveralls," said Lukowski earnestly.

"That reminds me," said MacNab. "I wonder if I could look over the invoices from your uniform company? We want to make sure all your coveralls are accounted for."

"Probably not," said Charles. "There always seems to be something missing. Mostly shop towels."

Miss Snow stepped forward with a file folder. "Here are the latest invoices," she said.

"Fine," said MacNab. "And yes, I have a warrant."

"But I'll need copies for my books," said Sylvia Snow, looking truly horrified. "There's a copy place at the end of the block. I can run out and—"

"I'll take care of that," said MacNab. "Maybe Dr. Carstairs here could come with us. Save everyone some time. We can talk to you while we go down there."

Charles followed them into the street. "I guess you're wondering if there was a blood-stained coverall," he said, shuddering.

The policemen ignored him. "Nice funeral, wasn't it Dr. Carstairs?" said Lukowski pleasantly.

"I suppose so," said Charles.

"Didn't expect to see *you* there," said MacNab. "Seeing as how you hated his guts and all."

84

"A lot of people there didn't care for Dr. Bateman," said Charles, trying not to sound too defensive. "It was just a matter of professional respect. As a matter of fact, I happen to know that Dr. Bateman had plenty of enemies."

"Is that so?" said Lukowski with interest. Charles felt sure Lukowski knew he was innocent.

Charles warmed to his theme. "That's right. Did you know about Larry de la Roque? Apparently he tried to strangle Dr. Bateman just ten days or so ago."

MacNab smiled. "That's right. But he was safely locked up in the state laughing academy before Bateman disappeared. And he didn't get out until yesterday. So he's alibied."

"Tough break for you," said Lukowski, with real sympathy in his voice.

"There were plenty of others," went on Charles, recklessly naming names. After all, had his colleagues rallied around him? "Dr. Smathers, for instance. He's running the department now. Why, I heard a rumor that Bateman had been holding a plagiarism charge over him."

"Really?" MacNab seemed uninterested.

"And Eleanor Zimmer hated him. And Bill Gunderson conspired against him. That department was a hotbed of hate, greed, and sin."

"That may be true," said Lukowski gently, "but we found Bateman's body in your garage. You have to understand our position, Dr. Carstairs. It means we have to check you out pretty thoroughly."

"Uncle Cosmo's garage," corrected Charles. "Boy, I wish I knew where he was. Really, if anyone at that garage killed Bateman, it's more likely to be my uncle than me. Not that I'm accusing him," he added hastily.

"Now let me get this straight, Dr. Carstairs," said Lukowski. "Are you saying you think your uncle did this?"

"Was your uncle fooling around with the wife too?" asked MacNab. They had reached the copy store, and MacNab handed over the invoices to a clerk. "One of each, please."

"Bateman *was* maddening. Maybe he complained so much about his tune-up that Uncle Cosmo just grabbed the nearest tool and hit him over the head." Charles was sure Uncle Cosmo could get off with involuntary manslaughter or something if this were the case. Plenty of people could testify as to how aggravating Bateman could be. Charles would be glad to do it himself.

"Hold it," said MacNab. "You're saying your uncle did this? Just lost it and hit him over the head?"

"Well, it's a slight possibility," said Charles. "If Uncle Cosmo did it, though, I'm sure it was an accident. Uncle Cosmo wouldn't kill anyone on purpose.

"Besides," added Charles, "I don't think he was even killed on the premises."

"How do you figure that?" said MacNab.

"The glass," said Charles. "The car had a good windshield when it was parked in the alley behind the shop. That's what Bud tells me. No one saw it for a while. Then it turned up again. But with the windshield smashed. And there's no windshield glass on the shop floor. Or outside in the alley where it was parked when Phil pushed it in."

"You're right there. And it's fairly clear the place hadn't been cleaned in weeks. In fact, you run a pretty filthy shop. Right now, it's one of the few little details that's saving you," said MacNab begrudgingly.

"And," said Charles triumphantly, "you didn't find any blood on the shop floor, did you?"

"Can't get a decent sample from concrete," said Lukowski. "The absence of blood stains doesn't mean a thing. The doctor tells us there wouldn't have been much blood. The perpetrator apparently brought down the weapon in such a way as to force Dr. Bateman's brains deeper inside his skull and—"

"Never mind," said Charles.

"So you're saying it never happened at that shop of yours, but that if it did your uncle probably did it," summarized MacNab. "Interesting theory."

"What about Mrs. Bateman?" demanded Charles wildly. "She's a strange woman, very dramatic. I wouldn't put anything past her."

"Wonder if she knows how to weld?" mused MacNab.

"Weld?" Charles was puzzled.

"Do you know how to weld?" said Lukowski.

"I took metal shop in high school. Did a little of it for my uncle, but mostly he sent that stuff out. Why?"

"Because," said MacNab, "the body was welded in the back of that Volvo. Weird, huh?"

"No wonder it was so hard to pop that trunk," said Charles, taken aback.

The three men had reached the door of Cosmo's Car Center. MacNab handed Charles the coverall invoices.

"Oh honestly," said Charles. "This is so absurd. If I wanted to kill Bateman, would I do it in such a stupid way? Leaving the body at Cosmo's Car Center? I'm not stupid, you know."

The detectives didn't answer him. "We'll be in touch," said Lukowski. "Don't leave town," added MacNab.

Scowling, Charles made his way back into the shop, wondering what new horrors awaited him. If only he could get in a few hours of wrenching at thirty-five dollars an hour, and make sure the other fellows did the same, maybe he could start to make some money.

When he went in he discovered Sylvia staring rather dreamily through the dirty front window. "You know," she said thoughtfully, "maybe some plants would be nice."

"Plants!" Charles practically exploded.

"I was thinking a window box with geraniums or something. It would look inviting."

"Let's wait until we get control of the business," he said.

"Look out there," she said.

"I'm not interested in window boxes," he said.

"No, I mean look at that green car out there."

Charles looked. A battered green Chevy Vega was parked across the street. Inside, partially obscured behind a newspaper, sat a man. All Charles could see of him was the top of a bald head and a beefy, freckled arm.

"He's been out there all morning," said Sylvia. "And I think I saw him poking around yesterday, too. Walking down the street."

"Wonderful," said Charles. "I guess we're under police surveillance." He turned back to her. "Geraniums! I can't believe you want to plant geraniums."

"Maybe some of those ornamental cabbages in winter. For a spot of color." She ignored his frustrated glare. "This could be a nice little business. With geraniums out front."

"The sooner I find out where I stand, the sooner I'll know what kind of a business this can be. How much am I paying you to find out, anyway?"

"Fifteen dollars an hour," said Miss Snow. "Of course, I only get half that."

"Yes, and I pay all of it," said Charles testily.

"I should have a complete statement for you this evening," said Sylvia, whose dreamy gardening persona seemed to disappear, replaced by something more brisk and businesslike. "After that, if you want more help, maybe we could make our own arrangements."

"We'll see," said Charles, preparing to go back into the shop and check on the boys before he went home and changed.

Sylvia raised her pencil in the air and said over her shoulder, "You aren't going back there without a coverall, are you?" in an irritating, arch way.

"I've already got to take the damned suit to the cleaners," snapped Charles.

Inside the work area he looked at the blackboard, where scheduled jobs were written, and was glad to see Steve had checked off two big jobs. Bud was still fumbling around under the VW van, and Phil was still looking puzzled under the hood of the car that had splattered Charles with oil.

Phil looked up, his pale face twisted with remorse. "Gee, I really am sorry about your suit. I feel so bad."

"It's fine, it's all right," said Charles. He didn't want Phil to burst into tears, so he went over to him and patted his arm. "No big deal. Really."

"I think I got this car figured out, though," said Phil happily.

"Oh yeah?"

"It's two problems, really. First of all, this battery here . . ." Phil gave the battery a light tap with a wrench, and then Charles saw something he'd only seen once before—an exploding battery. Phil leaped clear as sparks flashed. With a tremendous bang, the battery burst open. Charles jumped back to get away from the flying battery acid. He felt it stinging over his body from his chest to his knees, and ran immediately for the sink. If he was fast enough, he could rinse off the acid before it ate into his clothes.

He was, however, too late. By the time he reached the sink, where Steve was lounging and wiping off his hands, the acid had done its work and left a whole constellation of small holes in the fabric of his brother-in-law's suit.

CHAPTER
8

Lukowski and MacNab slid into their car. MacNab turned to his younger partner. "Well, what do you think?"

Lukowski frowned. "It's too bad we don't have any physical evidence."

"Don't worry. We'll nail him. Notice how he's trying to nail everyone else? Jesus. His uncle, the widow, all those other professors."

Lukowski smiled. "Yeah. De la Roque looked like a possibility, but he's cleared all right. Missing persons actually gave us a leg up on all this. Saved us a lot of time establishing the de la Roque alibi."

"I'm surprised they worked so hard," said MacNab thoughtfully. "Missing middle-aged married men are generally missing on purpose."

"Davis was pretty impressed with Mrs. Bateman. I guess she got to him, convinced him this was serious. Maybe that business about the mayor being at his banquet gave him an extra push."

"Let's see what they say about this Bateman up at the

university. And about our guy Carstairs.'' MacNab turned on the ignition and drove out into the traffic on Roosevelt. MacNab as senior partner could have had the unspoken privilege of being driven, but he hated to have anyone else drive him. Lukowski didn't care one way or the other. He liked MacNab, but he knew MacNab could be irritable, so he generally gave in to him on small matters, saving any real disagreement for important ones.

''That secretary there seemed real efficient,'' commented Lukowski as they entered one of the older Gothic en-crusted brick buildings on campus. ''Says she's got them all scheduled one after the other in the conference room. Except de la Roque. Apparently the boss doesn't want him on the premises, so if we think we need to talk to him we'll have to do it on our own. I got a good address on him.''

The department's senior secretary, Mary Ellen Robbins, had indeed arranged things expeditiously. She even had coffee set out for the policemen. A no-nonsense type in her early fifties, with a capacious bosom and wide hips, her iron-gray hair cut short and glasses dangling on a chain around her neck, she handed them a list of the faculty and announced she'd be sending them in in the order on the sheet.

''We really appreciate your setting this up so smoothly,'' said Lukowski.

Mrs. Robbins gave him a quirky little smile. ''Kind of fun to call them all here and tell them they have to show up when I say, because it's the police,'' she commented.

''You'd be surprised how little that means to a lot of people today,'' growled MacNab.

The first to be interviewed was Acting Department Chairman Smathers. A fussy little man, obviously nervous, who took a good deal of time before answering each question, he had little to tell the police. Roland Bateman, according to Smathers, was a wonderful man. He had no enemies. He was happily married to a lovely wife. Everything in the department was just fine, they were all one big, happy family.

"What about this de la Roque individual?" said MacNab.

Smathers removed his thick glasses and polished them. "Well, he's really no longer part of the department," he said, as if that ended the matter.

"Apparently he assaulted Bateman," said Lukowski.

"So I hear," said Smathers, "although I have no direct knowledge of the incident."

"And Professor Carstairs wasn't very happy with Bateman either, was he?" continued Lukowski gently, as if approaching a nervous rabbit.

'Well, I suppose not," said Smathers. "A nice enough young lad, worked hard, but Roland felt he just didn't have what it takes to be part of the work of a major university."

"Was Carstairs fooling around with Mrs. Bateman?" asked MacNab bluntly.

Smathers, who had replaced his glasses, removed them again and began repolishing them. "I really wouldn't know," he said. "Carstairs seemed to be the kind of young fellow women found attractive"—here he gave a little curl of the lip to indicate that this reflected poorly on the judgment of women—"but Mrs. Bateman, I'm sure, is above reproach."

Eleanor Zimmer arrived next. In her tight jeans, cowboy boots, and loose shirt, her face surrounded by a cloud of untidy hair, she had a careless, breezy manner that irritated MacNab. Lukowski, however, found it sexy.

Dr. Zimmer said Bateman was a pompous old bastard who managed to take in young, impressionable undergraduates and Dr. Smathers, but hadn't fooled her.

"Would anyone have wanted to kill him?" said Lukowski.

"Sure. But I can't think who would have. Larry de la Roque is probably crazy enough, but I guess he was locked up at the time." Lukowski and MacNab weren't in the habit of discussing their information on a case so they neither confirmed nor denied this.

"What about Dr. Carstairs?" said MacNab.

"He wouldn't kill anyone," she said. "But he had good reason. Bateman really screwed him over."

"How well do you think he got along with Mrs. Bateman?" said Lukowski.

"Who knows. I stayed away from the social side of things. Believe me, there's enough aggravation dealing with some of these people without actually socializing with them."

"I see," said Lukowski. "So you weren't at a party where Dr. Bateman was upset because of the attention Carstairs may have been paying to his wife?"

"No. But I think you got it wrong. Carstairs isn't exactly sexually aggressive. From what I hear, he just stands around looking good and gets jumped once in a while. I guess Mrs. Bateman had had a few drinks and hit on him. He didn't struggle."

"Do you think anything developed between them after that?" persisted Lukowski.

"Charles may be kind of a dope, but he's not that stupid," said Eleanor. "It was already too late, though. He was on Bateman's list, and so he was denied tenure."

When she'd left, MacNab said, "Okay, so maybe he wasn't screwing the wife, it was the tenure thing that set him off."

Bill Gunderson was next. Smiling and amiable, he had nothing to contribute about departmental animosities, and acknowledged only that he supposed the department secretaries may have gossiped about the faculty party where Carstairs and Mrs. Bateman were caught in a clinch. "I don't really have time to listen to the secretaries gossip."

Gunderson was, however, able to state that on Saturday the twelfth he had come in to do some work in his office and saw Dr. Bateman there. "We just chatted for a moment. He said he'd come by to pick up some papers, and was on his way to the grocery store. Then he was going to Cosmo's Car Center, where he'd apparently spent a lot of money on a tune-up that had left his car starting poorly and idling roughly."

"Did he say he had an appointment there?" said MacNab.

Gunderson looked pensive. "I can't really remember. He was real mad about the tune-up, though, and said he was going to have it out with that old crook Cosmo. His words, not mine. Then he made a few remarks about Carstairs having recommended the garage in the first place."

"When did he leave?" said Lukowski.

"It must have been about one-thirty or so. He was just here for a second. He'd had the secretaries type up some speech he was giving that evening, and he was picking it up."

When Gunderson left, MacNab said, "That makes it pretty clear. He left here around one-thirty and he never showed up to dress for that dinner at five. The doc couldn't tell us much, but he did say it could have happened on that Saturday."

The rest of the faculty had nothing new to add. The two men sensed only that Bateman hadn't been particularly well-liked, and one of the secretaries, a young blond named

JoAnne, seemed awfully cut up about the possibility that Charles Carstairs was a suspect. "Dr. Bateman was really mean to Charles," she said. "But I'm sure Charles wouldn't have hurt him. Dr. Carstairs is a real gentleman and a fine person."

When JoAnne had left, MacNab commented, "She has the hots for him all right. She should've taken some advice from that pushy Zimmer broad and just jumped him."

Finally, Mary Ellen Robbins came in. "That's the whole gang," she said. "Anything more we can do for you?"

"Maybe we could ask you a few questions," said Lukowski. "Can you think of any enemies Dr. Bateman might have had?"

She frowned thoughtfully. "I've thought about it a lot. Besides Larry de la Roque, who is a little, I guess you'd say, unbalanced, I can't think of anyone who had enough animosity to actually murder him."

"Dr. Gunderson says Bateman came in on Saturday the twelfth."

"That's right. He actually wanted me to drop off a speech I'd done for him to give that night, but my husband and I were going away for the weekend. And it wasn't even departmental work. So I made him come in and get it. The speech was gone on Monday, so I guess he did."

"There's been some gossip in the department about Dr. Carstairs and Mrs. Bateman," said Lukowski.

She shrugged. "Some little incident at a party. I heard about it. No big deal if you ask me, but Dr. Bateman was a very dignified man and he wouldn't have liked it."

"So you don't think Carstairs and Mrs. Bateman were having an affair?" persisted MacNab.

"I doubt it," said Mrs. Robbins. "To be quite honest, I think nothing would have happened at all if Dr. Bateman's wife hadn't had a few drinks."

"Exactly what kind of a drinker *is* Mrs. Bateman?" asked Lukowski.

"She drinks too much at parties," said Mrs. Robbins flatly. She lowered her voice. "I happen to know she had her license yanked after she was pulled over in one of those New Year's Eve dragnets. Six months."

Mrs. Robbins began to relish her topic a little. "She is kind of a dramatic women, you know, very difficult. Dr. Bateman would never say a word against her, but I sensed that he worried about her. That awards dinner, for instance. He had me answer the invitation to that and say Mrs. Bateman wouldn't be going. I think he was afraid she'd have too much to drink and act, well you know, vivacious."

"Wonder how Mrs. Robbins knew about Mrs. Bateman's DWI," mused Lukowski, as they were leaving the building. "Bateman wouldn't have wanted that blabbed around the department."

MacNab shrugged. "Can't keep anything from one of those sharp older gals in offices. Especially if she's handling your personal business too. Sounds like Mrs. Bateman got horny when she drank."

"Also sounds like Carstairs didn't take advantage of the situation," said Lukowski.

"Could be," said MacNab. "But maybe someone else did. We'd better put a surveillance on Mrs. Bateman. Maybe she's got a boyfriend crazy enough to have killed her husband."

CHAPTER
9

"I'M sorry, there's nothing we can do." The moon-faced woman looked at him triumphantly over her glasses.

"Just look at this." She poked at the fuzzy holes. "We can't perform miracles, you know."

"All right, I just thought I'd ask." Charles's teeth were clenched.

"Completely shot," continued the woman, with obvious relish.

"Okay, okay," said Charles. "It's shot. Fine."

"A real shame too. It's obviously an expensive suit." She flipped open the front of the jacket and examined the label.

Charles grabbed both pieces from her and turned on his heel, but not before he caught a parting sneer. Whether the sneer was for his carelessness in ruining the suit, or his ignorance of the technical limits of reweaving, he wasn't sure.

"I'll give it to charity," he said, trying to get some dignity back from the encounter. "Some mission downtown or something."

She didn't answer, having turned away from him to paw through some plastic-encased garments on hangers behind her.

Why, Charles wondered to himself, *did she take such obvious pleasure in being unable to help me?*

Suddenly, Charles felt a great surge of insight. Anyone with the proper bedside manner ought to be able to make a fortune in any service business. Fixing cars or reweaving holes was only a tiny part of it. If he could get the customers to believe that he cared about them and their cars, why, he could make himself a fortune. And why shouldn't he?

As soon as he found out what shape the business was in, he'd get to work and turn it around. He couldn't remember feeling so optimistic any time since he'd lost tenure and been saddled with the corpse of Dr. Bateman. He must get right back to the shop, make sure the day's work was progressing, and find out what Miss Snow had come up with.

Thinking of Miss Snow led him to wonder just how much she had cost him so far. She had been terribly helpful, filling in with all sorts of clerical work and phone answering while he was getting adjusted and being grilled by the police, but he couldn't afford to keep her there indefinitely. He got into his car and sat there for a few moments, counting the hours on his fingers and multiplying by fifteen. He had closed his eyes in concentration, and when he'd given up and resolved to do it on the calculator back at the office, he opened his eyes again.

What he saw when he did, unsettled him. There, scowling at him from behind the wheel of a green Chevy Vega, was a man. From his freckled, beefy arms and bald head, Charles took him to be the same guy who had been staking out Cosmo's.

It was humiliating to have the police following him around. He started to get out of the car and go confront the man. He was framing some little speech meant to indicate that he was innocent of murder, as well as savvy enough to know when he was being followed, but by the time he'd emerged from his own car, the man in the green Chevy had cruised away.

Charles tried not to worry about being followed, unpleasant as it was. He checked his watch. What with the funeral, MacNab's interrogation, going home to change, and then the fruitless trip to the dry cleaner's, it was almost five o'clock. There wasn't much of the day left to salvage, and he drove quickly over to Cosmo's.

When he arrived, he was pleased to see Miss Snow handing over keys to a smiling couple, and graciously accepting a check.

"And don't forget," she said to them as they left, "our mechanic says no more thirty-weight oil. Use multigrade. And we'll expect you back in three months or three thousand miles for a final adjustment."

Charles scrambled into coveralls and went back into the work area. "How're we doing?" he asked.

"We're actually in pretty good shape," said Bud, who was leaning against the wall drinking a can of Fresca. "As soon as I finish my break here, I'll put that starter motor in the VW van. Phil needs a few more parts, but that Sylvia ordered them and called the customers and told them it wouldn't be ready until tomorrow."

"That damned transmission didn't get back from the rebuild shop 'til just now," said Steve. He pointed to a Toyota pickup. "I wanted to finish the job, but did I have what I needed? No. That's always the way it is around here. How do you expect a guy to do a good job when he's fighting poor management all the time."

"When did the customer expect it?" asked Charles.

"I don't know. That's not my problem," snapped Steve. Like some librarians Charles had known who resented the public for coming in and disturbing the careful arrangement of books, Steve seemed to relate well to the cars and resent their owners for coming into the shop and bothering him.

"They're supposed to be here at six," supplied Bud.

"Fine," said Charles to Steve. "I'll help you. We've got a little more than an hour. Let's get it up on that lift and team it."

Steve sneered. "I ride alone, *kimosabe*."

"Not tonight," said Charles firmly. "I want this done and ready by six. Is the clutch in?"

"Of course. I'm the only guy in the shop with the right tool for it, too."

"Okay, fine. I'll help you get the transmission aligned and you put the screws in the bell housing and the starter motor. Then I'll get the drive shaft set up and the trans mount in."

"I don't like people working on *my* jobs," said Steve.

"Yeah? Well, we can discuss your deep personal feelings and your future here after we get the job done," said Charles heatedly.

"Okay, I'll go get the fucking car," said Steve morosely. Phil went with him to help him push it over to the lift.

Charles took advantage of a free moment to check on Sylvia Snow's progress.

"I'm sorry. I've been spending a lot of time, er, running things," she said apologetically.

"I appreciate that," replied Charles, "but I do need to know where I stand."

101

"I'll stay as late as you'd like, and we can talk about what I've discovered so far," she said. "It'll be easier to finish up without a lot of interruptions. These phones keep ringing, and I've been writing up invoices. I hope that's all right. I used the old ones as a model. Your uncle was computing the sales tax all wrong, though. You see in the last session the state legislature changed the—"

"Never mind," said Charles. "I've got a transmission to get in."

"So you know how to work on cars?" she said.

"Of course I do. I'm not a *complete* idiot," snapped Charles.

Although, as he set to work on the Toyota pickup, he worried that his skills were pretty rusty. It might take him a while to get back up to speed.

Fortunately, however, the transmission went in smoothly. He and Steve spoke little as they worked. Bud and Phil threw all their tools into their toolboxes and left. Above irritating rock music, to which Steve crooned along, they could hear Sylvia Snow at work, the buzz of her calculator and the slow click of the paper as it worked its way out.

As Steve finally lowered the truck from the hoist, Charles stood at the sink squirting hand cleaner into his palms. He hoped to God that the transmission worked. "We use these rebuilders before?" he asked Steve.

"Yeah. Probably the best in town. One of the few things your uncle did right. They didn't cut him any deals, either."

"Well, I sure hope it runs right," said Charles with feeling. He checked his watch. It was ten minutes to six.

"It'll run. If you did *your* part right," said Steve. "You know," he added, "I'm a real independent guy. I don't like the idea of two mechanics working on a car together."

"Right now I'm more interested in what the customer wants," said Charles.

"I guess you do really know how to turn a wrench," said Steve, with the air of someone granting a huge concession.

Charles smiled a little to himself. "Why don't you test-drive it while I write the bill? Test it uphill, downhill, and on the freeway."

"Don't you think I know how to fucking test-drive a car?"

Charles smiled again. Steve sounded a little defensive.

Steve took off in the truck, burning rubber down the alley. Charles went into the office.

"You *do* know how to fix cars, don't you?" said Miss Snow.

"Of course. I already told you. Of course there's a lot of new technology that's come out since I worked for Uncle Cosmo. Microprocessors in the newer cars and so forth. But I've always had good mechanical aptitude. In fact, my high school counselor said I tested very well in that area. I even thought of engineering for a while in college, but . . ." Charles paused. He remembered changing his major because there weren't enough girls in engineering. It seemed a frivolous way to choose a major.

"It makes a big difference."

"What do you mean?"

"At thirty-five an hour, if we can get you back there working on cars, this place can be a lot more profitable. I'll have to recompute."

"What exactly are you doing?"

"Projections. I want to be able to tell you what you can make here. Of course, with just a few days work I can't predict everything. There are many variables."

103

It sounded like academic research, the way she was describing it. This made Charles very nervous. He knew how easy it was to fudge the data. And what Miss Snow was doing suddenly seemed more important than any academic research. This was real life. *His* life.

Steve came back into the shop, a big smile on his face. "Goes like a wet dream," he announced, as Miss Snow turned pale. "And I'm going to tell the customer just that."

"I'll tell the customer about the car," said Charles hastily. "As soon as I write up the invoice. They should be here any minute now." He tried to get Steve back into the shop.

"I'll do it," said Miss Snow. "If you just fill in the job and the hours. The procedure you've been using with the taxes isn't right. As a matter of fact, you may owe the state a considerable sum."

This sounded ominous, but Charles didn't want to hear about it now. "Go on home, Steve. I'll just sweep up back there. Come on."

Back in the garage, Charles began to throw grease sweep on the bigger spots and searched for the broom. Steve got out of his coveralls and washed his hands. "Why the fuck are *you* cleaning up?" he demanded. "You're the owner. You should be worried about getting me the parts I need for my jobs. What we need is a kid to come in here and keep the place clean. It's filthy around here." It was Steve's usual tirade, but it lacked the power of his former outbursts. Charles felt he might be beginning to reach the young man.

Steve now went over to his own car, parked near the open shop door. Like many mechanics, Steve drove an old beater that he intended to get into showroom shape some day. He opened the trunk and pulled out a sixpack.

"Hey, the day's over. Let's have a beer."

Charles didn't really feel like it, but he thought he should be gracious, so he accepted. The two of them leaned against the back of the shop wall in the alley and drank lukewarm beer.

As they gazed into someone's back garden, a rather charming spot full of overgrown lilacs and blowsy rose-bushes behind a sagging lattice fence, Steve said, "You know, things might be better around here with someone besides Cosmo in charge. No offense, Chuck, but your uncle was a real jerk."

Charles didn't deny this, so Steve continued. "If you look around the shop and see what business we're taking in and what we're passing up, you'll see we need better equipment—especially diagnostics.

"And nothing against those other guys, but I'm the only good mechanic you've got. In fact, I'm damn good."

"You seem to be real fast," said Charles while Steve took a pull on his beer.

"That Bud has got to go. He's so out of it. He's still ordering spark plugs for '54 Olds 88's. I mean, really, give me a break.

"And Phil, he's so weird. I expect him to go over the edge any day. The guy's a nervous wreck. I was watching him the other day. It took him three and a half fucking hours to replace a CV joint."

"What exactly *is* wrong with him?" said Charles.

"Got his brains fried during the Viet Nam War."

"Did he see a lot of action?" Charles thought with relief of his educational deferments.

"Folded shirts at Ford Ord. It was too much for him. He snapped. Maybe he did a lot of bad dope. Who knows? These older guys are hard to figure." Steve fished into his pocket and produced what appeared to be a marijuana joint. "Want to do a number?"

Charles shook his head. "Gotta go over the books with Miss Snow pretty soon," he said, hoping Steve wasn't indulging during working hours. But if cannabis could curb Steve's tendency to lash out with verbal abuse, maybe it would be better if he did.

Steve lit up and sucked in. Charles hadn't been around drugs for years, and the whole thing made him nervous.

"Well," said Steve now, "maybe things could work out around here. Maybe you can get it together."

"I'd like to have you as an employee," said Charles solemnly. "A happy employee."

They were silent for a moment. Charles remembered this about working in the shop. Unlike with academic conversations, one wasn't expected to talk all the time. Charles indulged in a pleasant vision of a contented Steve wrenching away, making lots of money for the shop. Maybe Steve wasn't such a bad guy after all. His language was foul, and he should be kept away from the customers, but maybe he could be socialized.

A little old lady in a print housedress and an apron came shuffling out into the garden opposite them. She was sweet-looking, with fluffy white hair, pink cheeks, and bright eyes. A robin in a lilac tree sang. It was a serene and pretty picture.

"Well, if it ain't the old witch herself," screamed Steve. "Come out here to put a spell on us?"

Charles was horrified. The old lady scowled and advanced toward the fence.

"Shut up, will you," whispered Charles to Steve. "Good evening, ma'am," he said politely to the woman.

"Don't 'good evening' me, you smarmy son-of-a-bitch,"

106

she replied. "I see you fellows are up to all your old tricks. Smokin' that dope again, huh? I've got a mind to call the cops."

"Go ahead," hooted Steve. "You're calling them all the time anyways."

"Shut up, will you?" repeated Charles softly.

"Aw, that's just Mrs. Scroggins. She's been giving us the business for years. Who do you think calls the city and has all our cars towed outa here? Where do you think all those city inspectors come from? She sics 'em on us."

Charles recalled the stern young woman who wanted him to install a bathroom for the handicapped. He went toward the fence. "I'm sorry if there have been some misunderstandings," he began mildly.

The old woman glared at him through rotting lattice. "You're all crooks," she declared. "Parking cars in my alley. Running a fire hazard of a shop. And that damn dog kept getting into my garden."

"What are you bringing that up for?" yelled Steve. "Corky's history, thanks to you. Every time we turn around, you're harassing us."

"I'm sorry to hear that," said Charles. "We're under new management, and I'm sure that—"

"This is Cosmo's nephew," explained Steve. "Chuck's in charge now."

"So you're that old bastard's nephew, eh? I've hated him ever since he offered me two hundred bucks for my valuable old Packard." She gestured at a dilapidated garage on her property. Charles knew that every mechanic thrilled to stories, probably apocryphal, of a neglected old classic car in some widow's garage that could be picked up for a song, restored, and auctioned off for a fortune. Apparently Uncle Cosmo had hoped to strike it rich this way. Typical, thought Charles.

"When I heard that bum won the lottery, it made me sick," continued the old woman.

"He's gone now," said Charles. "I'm here."

"Well, things aren't much better over there," she said rather wildly. "Now you're killing people and stuffing them in cars. If I hadn't been up at my daughter's that weekend, I'd probably be dead too. But I heard about you on the news. They say the poor stiff was welded in there. *Nothing* you people do surprises me." She shook her finger at them. "You boys oughta be ashamed of yourselves."

"She probably did it herself," said Steve with hilarity. "Conked that old professor for parking in the alley. Naw, she didn't do it. She can't weld."

"The hell you say. I can weld a straighter and neater bead than any of you bastards. Down in Long Beach, back in '43, me and the girls put together a whole Liberty Ship from keel to launch in one week." Abruptly, Mrs. Scroggins turned away from them, pulled a pair of pruning shears from her apron pocket, and began deadheading some early roses.

CHAPTER

10

"F ROM what you've told me," said Charles, frowning over the stacks of paper Miss Snow had laid out in front of him, "I'll be lucky if I don't go to jail."

"Now, don't panic," she said coolly. "It's not that bad. Lots of people owe the state money. And the other debts aren't that bad. If you can keep expenses down to the bone for a while, you can catch up."

Charles sighed. His euphoria of earlier in the evening had gone. It seemed Uncle Cosmo had no real assets, outside of a lot of junker cars, his elderly tow truck, and plenty of debts.

Miss Snow frowned over the figures. "But I have to repeat, we still don't know exactly everything. For instance there's the matter of rent. I found a couple of rent receipts, and the amount is certainly reasonable, but I don't know if he has a lease or with whom. The signature is illegible. And the tax information is a real shambles. I told you he hasn't been paying enough sales tax to the state, so that means you owe them a lot of money, and he's a couple of quarters behind on the money he's been withholding from the employees' checks.'' Miss Snow tried to explain the intricacies of payroll deductions, but Charles cut her off.

"You mean he's been taking money out of people's checks and using it himself?"

She shrugged. "Happens all the time. I guess he thought he could catch up when it came time to turn the money over to whatever agency was collecting the funds. Small businessmen often see those funds as a quick source of interest-free cash."

"How much behind *was* he on all this stuff?"

"It'll take me longer to find that out," she replied.

Charles was overwhelmed. He took a deep breath. "Tell me honestly, what would you do if you were in my position?"

She shrugged again. The gesture irritated Charles. It was as if his problems were all inconsequential. "That depends on a lot of things. What you want to do with your life. If you like the business. If you're any good at it. The mechanical part and the rest of it."

"I must admit, I'm kind of excited about the idea of making it all work," said Charles. "I mean, I like working on cars. I think I'd like to be helpful to people whose cars aren't running right. And I'd like to make a little money, too, for my trouble."

"I don't see why you shouldn't be able to make money," she said.

For a minute Charles thought he'd unburden himself to her about his academic career, but it occurred to him she might not want to sit around and listen, even for half of fifteen dollars an hour. After all, shrinks got a lot more than that.

Suddenly, Miss Snow leaned forward and swept an errant strand of dark hair from her smooth forehead. There was something intense about the gesture. "Listen," she said. "I'm not supposed to give the kind of advice you're asking for. I'm just supposed to get the figures all lined up for you. For that matter, I'm not supposed to answer phones and write up invoices and order parts either. But, strictly off the record, and you'd better not quote me to the temporary agency, I think you could make this work." She sat back, looking rather surprised that she'd said this much.

"Why can't you tell me what you think?" said Charles.

"I'm really just a bookkeeper. Not an accountant even, or a small business consultant. They'd get mad if they knew I did anything more than some simple book work. They charge more for the kind of services you need."

"Well what *do* you think?"

"Your uncle had a lot of unhappy customers, and he kept terrible records. If you got a handle on the financial part and improved the quality of the work, you could do just fine.

"You need someone to get all this old stuff figured out, set up priorities for paying old debts and taxes, and do some financial planning. And you need someone to take care of all the support functions while you fix cars, make sure the other guys fix cars, and deal with the customers."

She paused, and looked slightly embarrassed. "You know, I think you'd be good with the customers. You have a lot of charm. I mean, you're personable and you seem intelligent and, even though you've been under a lot of pressure what with Dr. Bateman and all, you seem very nice. That means a lot to someone with a broken car. I bet you could handle the customers nicely."

"Funny," said Charles. "That's just what I was thinking at the dry cleaner's today."

"I've said too much," she said. "I can't really tell you what to do."

"I'm actually a professor, you know," he said. "But that seems to have hit a snag. Maybe I could do this for a while. While I was looking for another appointment."

"I don't see what you've got to lose," she said. "You can't sell the business in the shape it's in. Of course, you're still teaching, aren't you?"

"As soon as spring break is over I will be. But I've only got two classes to teach. If I retread my old lecture notes, stiff the students a little on office hours, and forget about research, I'll have plenty of time." After all, thought Charles to himself, isn't that what people *with* tenure did all the time?

"There's just one thing," said Miss Snow. "This murder."

"Oh, I know that's pretty bad, public relations–wise."

"I was thinking about a worse possibility than bad PR."

"You mean—"

"Those cops seem to act like you did it." Miss Snow looked uncomfortable.

"But I didn't." Charles couldn't believe Miss Snow suspected him too. Why would she be sitting with him all alone in the shop if she thought he was a cold-blooded killer?

"I know you didn't, but until they find out who did, you might not be able to devote much time to the business. I mean, with your academic work and planning a defense or whatever . . ."

"Surely it won't come to that," said Charles, horrified.

"Look at it this way. Even if they don't arrest you,

someone here may be a murderer. I'd call that a pretty big personnel problem."

"You've got a point there," said Charles.

"How close were you to your uncle," she said delicately.

"Uncle Cosmo?" Charles wasn't sure. He'd liked him as a kid because Uncle Cosmo let him fool around with cars. Later, Uncle Cosmo had been glad to take him on. It made it a lot easier to get through school. "He was always nice to me. Uncle Cosmo was always looking to make a quick buck, but he was basically good-hearted. If you mean do I think he killed Dr. Bateman, no I don't think he could. And there's no reason he would kill Bateman." Charles didn't mention his scenario where Bateman infuriated Uncle Cosmo with some pompous remark and got hit hard on the head.

"I wasn't suggesting your uncle killed anybody," said Miss Snow. Something about her tone made Charles think she had been suggesting exactly that. "It's just that what with his big win and all, perhaps you could persuade him to help you clear up some of these old debts. Of course, if you're pulling in a salary as a professor while you're really working here, you should be able to clear up those debts."

Her unfortunate phrasing made Charles sound a little sleazy, but how could anyone outside of the academic world know how it worked? Why, professors were always writing books they hoped would become bestsellers and going off on junkets to read papers here and there while on salary. What was so different about this? Anyway, maybe Charles could do a study of the automotive culture. Get a paper out of it.

"Well, you've certainly given me a lot of think about," he said. "And you've done a lot of work here. I really appreciate it."

"Fine," she said brusquely. "Well I'll just gather up my things and you'll get the bill from the agency at the end of the month." She rose.

" But you're not leaving, are you?" he said, realizing at once how ridiculous he sounded. "What will I do without you? I don't know what to do next."

Sylvia Snow smiled and sat down again. "You really can't afford to pay the agency to have me come in and run everything for you," she said. "But I could take you on as a private client. Of course we couldn't tell the temporary people. But I only take those jobs when things are a little slow. Mostly I get my own jobs on a word-of-mouth basis."

"I see. Well I'm sure we can come to some arrangement. That is, if you think I can afford you."

"The way I see it," said Miss Snow firmly, "you can't afford not to afford me."

After discussing the details of her employment, Miss Snow gathered up her basket, rewrapped herself in her hairy blanket, and left.

Charles was tired and all keyed up. He should go home and rest. He was in no state to think logically about all the things on his mind. Just two weeks ago, his life had been serene and orderly. There had been no decisions to make, no horrible puzzle, like the mysterious death of Dr. Bateman, hanging over him. Who had killed him? Sylvia Snow had touched on an important point. Until *that* was cleared up, nothing else could really be cleared up properly.

He stared down at the desk for a moment, half tempted to take home all the papers she had prepared. Those figures, incomplete as they were, might tell him whether or not to go ahead and try to make the business work.

Suddenly, he heard the unmistakable sound of a key in a lock. Someone had entered the door that led from the work area out into the alley. Charles went back there and saw the silhouette of a short man in a hat in the open doorway. He fumbled for the light switch.

The man was a tough-looking specimen, lean and hard, with a weatherbeaten, tanned face. Besides a cowboy hat, he wore Western boots and jeans, and an expensive-looking sheepskin coat. Charles was reminded of the Marlboro man.

"Who are you?" he asked the man.

"Who are you?" The voice was belligerent.

"I asked first," said Charles. "I see you let yourself in with a key."

"Yeah. So what?"

They didn't seem to be getting anywhere. "I'm Charles Carstairs. I own the place."

"What happened to Cosmo?"

"He's my uncle. I'm running the business now," said Charles.

"I made a deal with Cosmo. He never told me about you. I use this place once in a while. Nights and weekends. When I'm in town."

Probably some guy who needed somewhere to work on his car. Charles decided he didn't need to make extra money running a rent-a-shop. "Yeah, well, I'm sorry, you can't use the place," he said. "And I'd appreciate having that key back."

"Listen, you didn't hear me. I said I had a deal with your uncle. And I already paid him up front. A hundred and fifty for in and out privileges for a month. So why don't you just back off." There was a horrible menace in his voice, and Charles grew nervous. What could this guy be doing in here that was worth a hundred and fifty bucks?

"What exactly do you need the place for?" he asked.

"Listen, I don't think you understand. I don't stand around answering questions. Just clear out. You'll never know I've been here in the morning."

Charles sized up the man's height and weight in relation to his own. The guy was a lot shorter, and thin too. But he looked meaner. Well, that was all right. If the guy kept ordering Charles around his own shop, he just might get meaner himself.

"Sorry," he said firmly, taking a step toward the man. "We're closed."

"Hey," the man held up both palms in a gesture that looked as if it were placating, but also managed to look threatening. "I don't think you want any trouble. I don't like trouble myself. That's why I carry a sawed-off shotgun in my truck."

Charles stepped back a pace and mentally calculated how much time it would take the guy to get out the door, into his truck, and back with a shotgun with which to kill Charles. "Listen," he said in what hoped sounded like a reasonable tone, "I've had a pretty bad day. I went to a funeral and ruined my brother-in-law's best suit and everything. And the cops have been all over this place and all over me, because someone's dead body was found here a few days ago."

"Cops, eh? Why didn't you say so? And a stiff too. What kind of a place have you guys been running here?"

"What kind of work did you plan to do here, exactly?" said Charles.

The man smiled, revealing big white teeth. "Little odometer work."

"Well, listen, I can't let you in here now. The cops—"

"Yeah, yeah, okay. I'll wait until things calm down here. But I'll come back later. I already paid Cosmo."

Charles was deciding whether or not to give the man a hundred and fifty dollars just to keep him away. Miss Snow had been very insistent that expenses should be kept to the bare minimum for a while. Suddenly, the man vanished.

"Wait a minute," said Charles, following him out the door. There was no truck in the alley. Instead, the man was driving away fast in a red GTO. Charles couldn't see much about the car except that it had a dealer's license plate attached, as they usually were, to the body with magnets. Damn. He'd wanted to try and get that key back.

There wasn't much doubt in Charles's mind what the man was using the place for. He must be a set-back man who rolled back the mileage on used cars. Charles had always heard they had to be small and thin men, with small hands, to enable them to crawl into the tight spot under the dash and do their work.

He locked up again, wondering why he bothered. Everyone in town seemed to be able to get in and out of the place.

Dr. Bateman's murder, he reflected, was the exact opposite of the classic locked-room puzzle of detective fiction. Anyone could have come in, found Dr. Bateman, and killed him. *If* Dr. Bateman had been killed on the premises. If only Uncle Cosmo would surface, maybe they could find out what had happened at the shop on that fateful Saturday.

Later, when Charles was home, he wondered if he should call the police and tell them about the set-back man. Maybe Dr. Bateman had stumbled into the shop, looking to drag Cosmo over the coals for his shoddy tune-up, and come across the set-back man. The latter did seem to be some kind of a sociopath. Why else would he be carrying on about shotguns?

On the whole, Charles discounted the idea. Bateman wouldn't have any idea what the guy was doing wiggling under the dash and shaving ten thousand miles off a car's life history. Besides, if Charles called the police, several unpleasant things could happen. Uncle Cosmo could get in trouble, and the shop could get in trouble. Another possibility was that the mysterious stranger with the shotgun would come and blow him away. Charles decided to change the locks and say nothing to the police for now.

CHAPTER
11

WHEN Charles arrived the next morning, Sylvia Snow was already at work. She seemed to be moving stacks of papers around and bristled with energy. Charles prepared to go back into the shop, but she stopped him. "We've got a lot of things to go over here," she said. "Sign these. Signature cards. I'll need to be able to sign on the account. Then I want you to go over these papers with me. They all require some kind of a decision. Do we really need all these, for instance?" She handed him a box of old lottery tickets, some of them mangled and greasy. "I keep finding them everywhere."

"I guess not," said Charles. "Uncle Cosmo already won his pile." He tossed the tickets into the wastebasket. "Now I see how he won," he added drily. "He reduced the odds by buying a million tickets."

"The mail came already," she said. "Mostly bills, but there's a postcard for you."

"Who's it from?"

She looked appalled. "I would never read any personal

correspondence.'' Charles had always felt postcards didn't count, but Miss Snow's standards were obviously higher. The card showed a view of Las Vegas by night in smudgy neon. It read: "Hope everything's under control. Had a hitch with the passports, cause your aunt lied about her age, so we're spending a little time here until we go to the Bahamas. Tell the guys to stop fooling around and get to work. Wish you were here, but if you can't be, I'm glad I am. So Long. Uncle Cosmo."

"This is wonderful!" Charles waved the postcard around. "Uncle Cosmo has been found. Now we can ask him a couple of questions."

"I guess we'd better call that detective," said Miss Snow. "He wanted to know if we found Uncle Cosmo. Of course, we haven't really found him." She took the postcard and examined it. "There's no return address."

"That's true. Well, it's a start, isn't it?"

Detective MacNab was interested in the postcard, and said he'd be right over to take a look at it. While they waited for him, Miss Snow presented Charles with a series of problems requiring decisions. When he pondered them she came up with her own solutions to the problems, all of which seemed reasonable, and to which he agreed.

"You can go ahead and decide this stuff," he said, but she persisted in going over every excruciating detail of the little land mines Uncle Cosmo had left for him to tread on, despite his protests that all these things made him nervous.

She suggested they tell the Better Business Bureau that they didn't have enough knowledge to discuss the complaint against them. "Just stall them," she advised. "They're not a court of law or anything."

She told him she'd call downtown and see if he really had to install a bathroom for the handicapped. She'd come across the material the city inspector had left and had come to the conclusion that Cosmo's didn't apply and was grandfathered, having been an auto repair shop for many years.

She asked his permission to write a note to the old bookkeeper, Mrs. Aldrich, firing her, and she asked if she could order some in- and out-baskets. She also tried to get him to make a few more collection calls, but he wriggled away and got back into the shop area, where the mechanics were arriving to organize the day's work.

MacNab arrived with Lukowski in tow. Sylvia called Charles on the intercom. Breaking off from his task of replacing a defective fuel pump, he wiped his hands on a shop towel and went into the office. The policemen looked him up and down, taking in the greasy coveralls. "Say, you do actually work on cars, huh?" said MacNab with surprise.

"Of course I do," said Charles indignantly. No one seemed to find this believable. "Why do you think I'm running a shop?"

MacNab asked if he could keep the postcard. "We'll see if it can be traced in Las Vegas. We'll run a check of all the hotels down there. I imagine your uncle will be in one of the better places, now that he's rich.

"While I'm here," MacNab continued, "I'd like to go over that list Bud gave me again. Is he here?"

Sylvia Snow hit the intercom and summoned Bud, who seemed delighted at the opportunity to chat. He sat down cosily on the sofa, apparently prepared for a long session.

"We've been having a little trouble finding out who exactly some of these individuals are," he said. "Mind going over with me again who knew about the hidden spare key?"

121

"Glad to help," said Bud. "Coffee? I'm kind of in charge of making the coffee around here." He went over to the machine and looked disappointed to see that the coffee was already made.

"I'll make the coffee from now on," interjected Sylvia. "That way you can do more important things, like fix cars."

Bud started to say, "But when Cosmo was here—" but MacNab cut him off. "Can we get to this list? Okay, number one. Gary. The upholstery man. Do you have a last name on him?"

"No. We just call him Gary. He comes by all the time, looking for work. We've used him a few times. He has a dog. And he's born again. You know, 'Praise the Lord this, Praise the Lord that.' "

MacNab looked impatient. "But he knew where the key was?"

"That's right. He came in one night and did a little job for Cosmo, and we told him where the key was 'cause no one was around."

"Hang on a minute," said Miss Snow, flipping through a large Rolodex file. "I've just finished sorting out a lot of business cards I found lying around. I think I put him under *U* for upholstery." She handed over a card to a grateful MacNab.

"Okay, now we're getting somewhere. How about Mickey? The detail woman?"

"Oh, she's great," said Bud. "Big, strong, strapping woman. Great detailer. Real butch. We had her in here a couple of times to detail cars, and we told her where the key was so she could get in and out."

Sylvia looked puzzled, so Charles explained. "Detailers clean cars perfectly, inside and out. It's a real art." Charles

122

conjured up a scene where the strapping Mickey ran into Dr. Bateman when he stopped by the shop and crushed his skull with a large tool in retaliation for some sexist remark.

Miss Snow flipped through her files and produced another phone number.

"Okay. And what about this guy. Melvin."

"Scrap metal guy. He comes by and picks up our scrap metal. We never call him, he just comes by and picks up whatever we have out in the pile. But one time he tried to take the old garbage can we hide the key under away, and found the key. We put it back and told him not to move the garbage can again. Usually we use the dumpster, but sometimes it gets full."

"Does this guy have a regular route?" asked MacNab.

Bud shrugged. "I guess so."

"What does he look like?"

"Black," said Bud. "All the scrap guys are black. Big guy. Middle aged."

"Okay." MacNab frowned. "And the other individuals on the list we've found. Those two guys at Hi-Tech Auto up the street. And the used-car lot down the street. Are you sure this is everyone who knew about the key?"

"Gee, I think so. Of course maybe the uniform man knew. And some of the parts runners. And maybe that guy who fixes windshield nicks. I don't think so, though."

Charles rolled his eyes. It was a wonder the place hadn't been ripped off. He had to change those locks. For a second he thought he'd better tell the detectives about the set-back man, but then he changed his mind. Why open up that can of worms? He'd at least wait until he could talk to Uncle Cosmo about it.

"I hope you find Uncle Cosmo soon," he complained to MacNab. "I can't believe you haven't found him yet. I trust that now you know he's in Las Vegas you can talk to him.''

"Shouldn't be too hard to find a guy who gets a monthly check from the state," said MacNab. "There's no need to go off half-cocked."

Charles turned toward Lukowski, who seemed so much nicer, and said, "Do you have to have such conspicuous surveillance of the place? It makes me feel like a criminal." He gestured out the window, where the burly, freckled man sat in his car, buried in a copy of *USA Today*.

MacNab peered out into the street. "What the hell's he doing here?" he demanded of no one in particular. He strode out of the shop and across the street. MacNab opened the door of the green Chevy Vega and pulled the occupant by the collar out into the street. "Okay, Ferguson," he said through clenched teeth. "What's going on?"

Bud and Charles, who had followed MacNab out, stared in fascination.

"Nothing," said the man, obviously intimidated.

"Hanging around a murder scene, like a vulture. What are you trying to do? Solve the crime and try to collect any future reward? Or do you have a client?"

"Hey," said the man sharply. "Leave me alone or I'll file charges. Excessive force. I'm just an honest citizen minding his own business."

"You wouldn't get anywhere with any charges. Don't make me laugh."

"Yeah, but the paperwork and the hassle will keep you out of action for quite a while." The freckled man gave a little smirk.

"This man is not a police officer," said MacNab to Charles. "Not any more."

Charles reflected on TV police shows he had seen, and stared at Ferguson. "You mean he was a bad cop?"

124

"No, just a stupid one," said MacNab. To Ferguson he said, "I'd appreciate not seeing you around here."

Ferguson gave Bud and Charles a few curious glances, then got into his car and drove away.

"Calls himself a private investigator," said MacNab with disgust.

"Why didn't you tell him you'd yank his license?" said Bud, who obviously watched TV crime shows too.

MacNab gave him a withering glance. "An orangutan can get a license to be a detective in this state," he said.

Lukowski came out and the two policemen left, Lukowski with a polite "Good-bye," MacNab with an irritating "Don't leave town."

Back in the shop, Charles told Miss Snow he planned to change the locks.

"Good idea," she commented, and grabbed the yellow page directory. Charles had an idea. "After you look up locksmiths," he said, "see if you can find a private detective named Ferguson. He's the guy that's been watching us. I'd sure like to know why."

Miss Snow's eyes widened. Charles sensed that she found something thrilling about the goings-on around the shop. Well, that was just fine for a repressed bookkeeper with not much happening in her life. He personally would have preferred everything to be a little quieter, with no dead bodies littering up things.

Steve came slamming out into the lobby. "Okay. Who fucked up? These aren't my parts." He set a large box down heavily on the counter. "And where are my parts, I wonder? How the hell do you expect me to get anything fixed if I don't have the goddamned parts?"

Charles inspected the box, and saw a label that said *Hi-Tech Auto*. "Oh, these must be for the guys up the street," he said. "Maybe they got our order. I'll go check."

Actually, Charles welcomed the opportunity to nose around the Corsican brothers' place. After all, they were on the list of people who could get inside Cosmo's. Charles was rather depressed when he arrived at the rival shop. In place of a sagging green plastic couch and some old hunting magazines, the waiting area at Hi-Tech Auto had brown leather Barcelona chairs, healthy-looking rubber plants, and glass-topped table with *Architectural Digests* laid out in a neat, overlapping line.

The perky blond receptionist looked like an aerobics instructor. She was talking to a couple of customers, a tan lean man with capped teeth and Italian shoes and a rangy-looking woman with matching teeth and tan and a provocative version of the female power suit. They looked like rich realtors.

"We really need that car," the man was saying intensely. "I mean now. And we want all the extras too."

The two phrases seemed antithetical. Charles had the impression they might take a while, so, carrying his box of parts, he went back into the shop area. Here he was startled to see one of the Corsican brothers carefully folding up a plastic bag full of white powder and Scotch-taping it inside the glove box of a brand-new Porsche.

He pretended he hadn't seen anything, and handed over his box, exchanging it for one addressed to Cosmo's. As he left, the couple in the lobby were receiving their keys and flipping over an American Express card hastily. It was clear they were so eager to get into the car and inhale part of the contents of that plastic bag that they wouldn't ask any annoying questions about the bill or what had been done to the car—if anything. The Corsican brothers had certainly come up with a profitable sideline.

Back at Cosmo's, after mollifying Steve with his parts,

he prepared to get to work on the fuel pump switch, but Sylvia Snow stopped him. "I got ahold of that detective through his answering service," she said, thrilled. "He was at a phone booth near here, and just called in for his messages. I hope it's okay with you—I went ahead and arranged a meeting. He said he'd be glad to tell us why he was staking out this place. For cash of course."

"That should be interesting," said Charles.

"Come on," said Sylvia. "I arranged for us to meet him at that café on the corner. He said to make sure MacNab was gone. What do you think he knows?"

Charles had been right. Miss Snow was eager to play Nancy Drew. He supposed he'd have to let her accompany him to the meeting, although her time would have been better spent answering the phone.

When they arrived at the coffee shop, they spotted Ferguson in a corner booth, hunched warily over a mug of coffee. They slid into the bench opposite him.

"First of all," said Ferguson, "I charge one hundred an hour. I figure this little chat will take about half that." He paused. Charles opened his wallet and took out a twenty and a ten. Sylvia Snow was able to come up with the balance, and mentioned something about running this through petty cash.

"We just wondered why you were watching us," said Charles.

"It's about my car," said Ferguson. *Oh, no, not another unhappy customer*, thought Charles. Ferguson continued. "A couple—three weeks ago I was on a divorce case. 'Course that business has been dried up by this no-fault crap, but every once in a while you find someone who wants to have peace of mind about his or her spouse, you know what I mean?"

Charles wished the man would get to the point. He nodded. "Yes. Go on."

"So I was following this guy and he goes to the airport and gets on a commuter flight to Spokane. I stay right with him. I get on the plane too. The client is willing to pay all expenses. The only trouble was, my car is double parked out front. When I get back a few days later, it's been towed away. My client's good for it, but I have a little problem collecting right away."

"Poor cash flow," said Miss Snow sympathetically.

"You got that right. Anyway, when I finally get the scratch together to go bail out my car, I find out it's been towed to some wrecking yard. Sold for scrap. Can you imagine that? It's a real racket. I go in there and try to get my car back. I'm even willing to buy it back. But they wanted too much for it. Say it'll be crushed. I didn't like their attitude and I had a set of keys, so I eyeballed the thing in line to be crushed—they got one of those cubing machines, you know?"

Charles nodded, wondering what in God's name any of this had to do with Cosmo's Car Center.

"So I decide I'll go back at night. Feed some barbiturates in hamburger to the dog they got there, jump the fence, and drive my car home. Possession is nine tenths of the law, right? They want hassles, they can hassle me while the car is in my possession. It gets cubed, there's not much left to discuss."

Ferguson paused and drank coffee. "I already figured it'd be easy. I know a thing or two about burglar alarms, and I've already spotted this one as a dummy. All the labels and tape and stuff, but not connected. There's a lot of dumb bastards rely on that."

Charles winced. He had the same setup at Cosmo's.

"So I come back at night, all set to go reclaim my property, which I felt and still do feel is my own rightful, legal property that's being held illegally, and I see there's someone else there. In the middle of the night. So, while I'm standing there, wondering what to do, some guy gets in *my car* and drives away in it. Takes it out of the line of cars ready to be crushed. I get in and try to follow him, but I lose him up in the north end somewhere."

"Okay, then what happened?"

"Well," said Ferguson, leaning back in the manner of a great armchair detective. "Something's funny around that place. I figure those crooks up at the wrecking yard are pulling some kind of scam. They say they're going to crush my car, and then in the middle of the night someone drives it off. I want to get to the bottom of it all, so whenever I'm free, and after I get myself a new car, I stake the place out at night. Maybe I can figure out what they're up to. Or maybe the guy will come back, the guy who stole my car, and I can try and get it back from him. 'Course I didn't see him well, but you can recognize someone by the way he moves. I got a general idea of his build and age. Young guy. Wiry."

"What does any of this have to do with us?" said Charles, gritting his teeth.

"Well, on one of my stakeouts I see a truck pulling out of there. In the middle of the night. Can't tell who's behind the wheel, or what they've been up to, but I figure they might have something to do with my car."

"Yes?" said Charles encouragingly.

"It was your truck."

"My truck?"

"A tow truck. It said 'Cosmo's Car Center' on the side. So I wondered if you people had anything to do with my car." He leaned over to Charles. "If you know where my car is, I want it back."

"I don't know anything about your car," said Charles. "And I don't know what our tow truck would have to do with any of this."

"When was this?" said Sylvia.

Ferguson reached into his pocket and came up with a notebook. "Two Saturdays ago," he said.

Charles and Sylvia looked at each other, startled. That was the day Professor Bateman had disappeared.

"Let me get this straight," said Charles. "You saw our truck pulling out of this place. Not towing anything? Who was driving?"

"I don't know," said Ferguson. "No, it wasn't towing anything, and yes, it was pulling out. I couldn't turn around fast enough to follow it. I just figured there was something funny going on at that wrecking yard and you guys might know about it. I thought I'd see if you were running a stolen car ring or something."

"Well, are we?" said Charles. Nothing would surprise him.

"Can't do much of anything, what with the cops all over you, now can you?"

"What is the name of the wrecking yard?" asked Sylvia Snow.

"Elwood's. Right near the city limits up north."

The name sounded familiar to Charles. He'd ask Bud about it.

CHAPTER

12

CHARLES had a chance to ask Bud about it the next morning. Bud had welded a gas tank, and before replacing it in the car he took it out into the alley, leaned it against the building, and was hosing it off. "What do you know about Elwood's Auto Wrecking?" Charles asked him.

"Elwood was a real good friend of your uncle's." Charles was annoyed with the slow, lazy way Bud was training the hose on the gas tank. Charles was also disquieted by the fact that Bud was using the past tense when referring to Uncle Cosmo. Until that postcard had arrived yesterday, Charles had fleetingly worried that something awful had happened to Uncle Cosmo.

"As a matter of fact," said Bud, "when old lady Scroggins sicced animal control on us and made us get rid of Corky, why, old Elwood took him in."

"What do you know about his business? Is it legit? I mean is everything on the up and up?"

"Compared to what?" said Bud.

Charles didn't want to get into varying degrees of morality as practiced in the automotive trade. "Do you think they could have been stealing cars or something?"

Bud frowned and made new patterns of water on metal. "No, I don't think so. Elwood's sitting pretty without doing anything crooked. That old junkyard of his is on a nice piece of land. Some slick developers are going to put up condos there, and Elwood should make a lot of money. That's why he scraps pretty near every car he gets. It doesn't pay for him to be parting everything out when he's trying to clear off the land for the developers. While they get all the permits and red tape and stuff taken care of, old Elwood just smashes up everything that comes his way. He doesn't even care about the price of scrap."

Charles, convinced now that the stream of water had somehow hypnotized Bud, who was rinsing off a perfectly clean gas tank, went over and turned off the faucet. "You certainly are a mine of information," he said.

Bud looked startled that the hose he held no longer had water coming out of it, but he didn't change his position. "Well that's the story Fast Eddie told me, anyway. He works for Elwood. Drives him nuts, working for old Elwood.

"Haven't seen Fast Eddie lately. Phil does a lot of front-end work for him. Eddie turns over cars now and then."

Charles understood this last phrase. Turning over cars meant fixing up old junkers and selling them at a profit. He took it that Phil had ceased moonlighting and that was why Fast Eddie hadn't been around lately.

Gently, Charles removed the hose from Bud's hands. "Why don't you go inside and find something to do while this gas tank dries off. Check the brakes in that Datsun."

"Okay," said Bud.

Bud went back into the shop, and Charles coiled up the

hose and went over and investigated the old tow truck that was parked in the lot. Cosmo had had it for years. Charles had always loved riding around in it when he was younger. There were no keys in the ignition, but Charles imagined it would be easy enough to hot wire. For that matter, it would be easy enough for anyone to take the keys off the board in the office and drive it around. What had it been doing up at Elwood's the night Dr. Bateman presumably had died? Who had been at the wheel? Charles sat pondering this for a while, and wondered if he should tell MacNab and Lukowski what the private detective had revealed. It might have a bearing on the case. He hesitated because he wanted to know just what had been going on up at Elwood's. If Cosmo's Car Center were somehow involved . . .

His thoughts were interrupted by the sight of a large black man in coveralls who was leaping down from an old pickup with plywood sides. This must be the scrapper Bud had told the police about. With agility and speed that belied his size, the man began throwing the stack of old fenders and other parts leaning against the dumpster into his pickup. Then he rummaged through the dumpster itself. Charles, behind the tow truck, was unobserved. A second later the man made a final sprint over to the gas tank that lay drying in the sun and heaved it into his pickup. Then he leaped behind the wheel and set out.

Charles scrambled out from behind the tow truck. "Hey!" he yelled. "Don't take that! It's not scrap." The man didn't seem to hear and took off. Charles, computing the cost of a new tank for the customer's car, went off down the alley after him. Puffing, he caught up with the truck when it stopped behind Hi-Tech Auto. "Stop!" he shouted. "You took that gas tank. Give it back!"

"Say what?" said the scrap man, as he threw a chrome bumper onto the top of the pile in his truck. It made a horrible sound as it hit the gas tank.

Charles climbed onto the truck and tried to fish it out.

"Get off my truck," said the scrap man.

Charles explained about the gas tank, and the scrap man said, "Finders keepers. That's how my business works."

"But it doesn't belong to me. It's a customer's."

"How am I supposed to know? You people are always throwing out perfectly good stuff. Why, I found a bottle of fine wine, French, in there last week or so. *And* a good steak, a lipstick, a bottle of that Worcestershire sauce, and some cans of artichoke hearts. I drank the wine, but I gave the steak to my dogs, not knowing how long it'd been there. My wife said the lipstick was the wrong color, and I haven't found a use for the artichoke hearts yet either."

"They're nice in salads," said Charles, who was now struggling with the bumper. The scrap man came to help him.

"There were paper towels and lettuce too. It's just criminal, the waste that goes on in this country," the big man said crossly. He wrenched the gas tank out of his truck and threw it over the side.

From inside Hi-Tech Auto, one of the Corsican brothers came out to observe the scene. "Ha!" he said in his strange accent. "So this is where Cosmo's gets its high-quality used parts." He laughed maniacally. Charles, squatting on the ground checking the gas tank after its jettisoning, ignored him, choosing instead to address the scrap man.

"Thanks a lot," he said sarcastically, inspecting several dents. He hoped the welds were still good and that the tank would fit back in the car despite its new shape.

It wasn't until he'd struggled back up the alley carrying

the battered part that he wondered about that fine wine, steak, and the artichoke hearts. The police had said Dr. Bateman was doing a few errands before he disappeared. Dr. Bateman made it a point of honor to drink French wines, insisting that domestic wine was overrated. Had his groceries somehow ended up in the dumpster?

It could only mean that Bateman had been at Cosmo's the day he was killed. Charles had been eager to have it happen *off* the premises.

Seized with a desire to find out more about Dr. Bateman and the night of his death, Charles went into the office, stopping just long enough to hand Bud the dented gas tank. "Here, put this back in," he said. Steve stared at the slightly mangled part and said, "How the hell do you expect him to put that thing back in the goddamned car?" But Charles went past him.

"I'm going to take a look at that wrecking yard Ferguson told us about," he said to Sylvia Snow.

"Oh, can I come too?" she said pitifully. "After all, I was there when Mr. Ferguson told us about it. I'm dying to see it."

Charles ground his teeth, then decided it might be nice to have some company on the long drive up to the north end of town. Besides, he always got lost up there. Something told him Sylvia Snow never got lost.

"I'm going on a parts run," he said into the intercom. "Sylvia'll be coming with me. Bud can answer the phone."

"What do you need Sylvia for?" said Steve in a nasty voice full of innuendo.

Sylvia depressed the intercom switch. "So I can learn how to run for parts, you jerk," she said. "You're always complaining about parts availability."

"I'm sorry," she whispered to Charles. "Steve has been driving me crazy."

They continued their conversation in the car. "I know he's a pain," said Charles. "I guess I should get rid of him."

"No way," said Sylvia firmly. "I've been keeping track of productivity, and that creep is carrying the whole place."

"There are some awfully nice things about academia," said Charles wistfully. "There, you can sometimes get rid of people even if they are productive, just because they're jerks. No bottom line to worry about."

"I can't see why you, of all people, should find that advantageous," she replied. "Isn't that what happened to you?"

"I guess it is," said Charles thoughtfully.

"Not that you're a jerk," added Sylvia hastily.

"No, of course not."

Charles wasn't sure he knew what he had expected up at Elwood's. The place looked like a perfectly normal wrecking yard. He decided he'd pretend he was looking for an obscure part, and he and Sylvia went into the office; but before they did, Charles spotted a car behind the barbed wire fence. It was a '75 Pinto. "Hi," he said to the sour-faced man behind the counter. "You must be Elwood."

"That's right."

"I'm Charles Carstairs, Cosmo's nephew. I took over the business." He also introduced Sylvia.

"Guess your uncle forgot about his old friends when he made his bundle," said Elwood. "He didn't come by or nothing. Just took off."

"Well," said Charles boldly, "I guess you'll be coming into a pile yourself, once you sell this land."

"What can I do for you?" said Elwood, apparently reluctant to discuss his own good fortune.

"I'm looking for a rear seat for a '75 Pinto," said Charles. "I notice you got one of them back there in the lot."

"Yeah. Planned on scrapping it, but I guess I can sell you that rear seat."

A tall, skinny youth with a baseball cap and an unfashionable length of greasy hair hanging down from beneath it came into the office. "Eddie, this guy wants the rear seat in that '75 Pinto we got back there. Help him, will you?"

Sylvia and Charles followed Eddie, picking their way across ground littered with screws and bolts and through piles of cars in various stages of cannibalization and deterioration. Looming overhead was a large auto crusher. Intermittently it made a hideous sound of crunching metal and glass as its powerful arms folded cars in on themselves. The hydraulic mechanism made an almost human heaving sound, as if it worked with great effort.

To one side, chained to a large stake and pawing at the scrabbled dirt beneath its paws, was a vicious-looking German shepherd. The late lamented Corky, Charles presumed, waiting until nightfall to be let out and patrol among the ghosts of old cars.

The depressing atmosphere gave Charles one happy thought. His own situation could have been worse. Uncle Cosmo could have given him a wrecking yard in which to spend the rest of his days.

"Up there," said Eddie laconically, indicating the Pinto perched on top of a stack of old cars. "Go ahead and take a look."

Charles sighed. Why had he chosen such an inaccessible

part, not to mention large and presumably expensive? He began to climb up the tower of cars, inserting his feet through broken windows to get a foothold. Sylvia Snow must have had similar thoughts, because she said, "Make sure it's in good condition."

"Thanks for reminding me," said Charles. He peered into the rear of the Pinto. The seat looked perfect. "Too bad," he shouted down to Eddie, "wrong color."

He climbed down, trying to think of a way to engage Fast Eddie in conversation. "We're looking for a couple of other body parts," he said. "Got an older Volvo around? 140 Series?" It was the first car that popped into his head, probably because it was the model in which Dr. Bateman had been found.

Fast Eddie reacted. His taut body seemed to grow tauter, as if ready for some blow. His eyes narrowed. "Nothing like that," he said, fishing in his shirt pocket for a twisted cigarette pack.

Charles watched him work a cigarette out and light it. After he'd hunched over the match and drawn himself back, exhaling, he looked calm again.

There was no doubt in Charles's mind. Fast Eddie had reacted.

"Guess that's Corky," said Charles affably, indicating the snarling, mangy animal. "He used to be my uncle's dog. Uncle Cosmo. I'm Charles Carstairs, I run the business now. And this is Sylvia Snow."

"How do you do?" said Sylvia. Charles realized they made a rather incongruous little group standing out among the rusting hulks being polite. Fast Eddie seemed to think so too.

"So what do you guys want, anyway?" he said with a trace of belligerence and more than a little curiosity.

"Just looking for a few deals on used parts," said Charles.

"Okay. Well, look around." Eddie turned and left. They watched him walk away.

"He's very graceful, isn't he?" said Sylvia.

"Graceful! He acts like a thug."

"I mean the way he moves," she said. "He could have been a dancer." She seemed to sense that Charles found this remark odd, and said, "I used to dance. I just notice things like that." She looked around the wrecking yard and winced as the auto crusher wheezed and crumpled. "Let's get out of here," she said. "This place gives me the creeps."

CHAPTER
13

"READY?" MacNab had put on his loudly checked sportsjacket and hovered impatiently over Lukowski's desk. Lukowski, hunched over the phone, gestured at him impatiently. "Yeah. Okay. He'll say so? Great." He put down the receiver. "That was the auto detail. They found the junkman. You know, the black guy. And bingo."

"What do you mean?" MacNab looked perplexed.

"The junkman says he found a bag of perfectly good groceries in the dumpster behind Cosmo's Car Center." Lukowski consulted his notes. "A good steak. French wine. A can of artichoke hearts. Paper towels. A lipstick. Lettuce. A bottle of Worcestershire sauce. All we have to do is ask the widow what was on that shopping list and we place Bateman at the shop. All that crap about the windshield, about the car not being there, Carstairs can forget it. Bateman was there."

"Carstairs iced him and pitched his groceries in the dumpster," said MacNab with satisfaction. "Terrific."

Lukowski rose and put on his own jacket over his

shoulder holster. "A good defense attorney could have made a big deal about reasonable doubt with that car having been missing from the premises. That Bud sticks to his story that the Volvo had been towed away. But the prosecutor can say the city didn't tow it, and he can put Bateman's groceries there."

"Any problem with the junkman testifying?" said MacNab.

"No problem. Apparently the guy is really pissed that someone would throw out a lot of good stuff. Can't wait to get on the stand and carry on about waste."

"Hey, terrific," said MacNab, patting Lukowski on the shoulder. "We'll get all our ducks in a row on this real fast. You'll see. Come on, let's go talk to that lady banker. She was real cagey on the phone, you know, sounded afraid to talk to a cop, but she says she has some info on that Cosmo character. Maybe he's been writing checks and she knows where he is."

"Let's go take care of that right away," said Lukowski.

"I'd like to get this whole deal cleared up fast," said MacNab. "I promised the wife that we're taking that vacation, and no screw ups this time."

The two men left the office and drove to a bank branch in the University District. They had an appointment with Debbie Olson, an officer of the bank who had handled Cosmo's Car Center business and who had called, indicating she had information pertinent to the case.

They found Ms. Olson behind a plaque bearing her name. She was showing a frowning old man a book with various styles of checks. "And here's a Pacific sunset," she said. "Very attractive."

"I just want plain checks," said the man. "No fruit

trees in bloom, no sunsets, no smiling faces, just some plain checks.''

"All right,'' said Ms. Olson huffily. "Most of our customers like something cheerful.'' She slammed some plastic-covered sample books around. "If you want something more traditional we can do that too. Here's something with just a simple crest.''

"It's not my crest,'' snapped the old man. "If I wanted a crest I could send money to some outfit in Ohio and get a plastic wall hanging with a crest on it. They advertise in *TV Guide*.''

Lukowski surveyed Ms. Olson, a well-built blond in a dress-for-success suit with a polyester sheen to it. Everyone was an executive these days.

The two men waited patiently for a moment while the old man scrutinized some checks, debating the merits of blue versus green, then MacNab muscled in, flashing his badge and insinuating his bulk between Ms. Olson and her customer.

Debbie Olson arranged for someone else to guide the customer through the intricacies of opening a checking account. "Tell him about the free monogramming on the checkbook cover,'' she instructed her replacement, before turning her attention to the officers.

"Let me just find Mr. LaRue, our branch manager,'' she said. "He wants to be in on the meeting.''

"What exactly did you want to tell us?'' said MacNab impatiently.

She gestured nervously to a thin, balding man in gray, who bustled over. After introductions were made, the bankers led the policemen into a small conference room. More time was taken up with the presentation of business cards. Mr. LaRue's read *Branch Manager*, Ms. Olson's *Customer Relations*.

"I'm sorry gentlemen," began LaRue, "that Ms. Olson here contacted you on her own. As a representative of the bank she should have gone through proper channels, and I should have called you, after conferring with my superiors, of course. It's all spelled out in the policy manual," he said severely to Ms. Olson. "Under 'contacts with non-bank agencies.' "

Lukowski imagined Mr. LaRue thumbing through the manual as someone bled to death in his bank, wondering whether or not to call an ambulance. "Why did you call us, Ms. Olson?" he said patiently.

"Well," she said, "it's just that I saw on TV how you were looking for Mr. Sweeney, Cosmo Sweeney, that is. And I thought you should know that he was at a bank-sponsored workshop all day."

"What day?" said Lukowski.

"The Saturday Dr. Bateman disappeared. I mean, the newspaper said he'd been last seen on the twelfth. And that was the day I ran the small business cash flow workshop. And Mr. Sweeney was there all day. From nine-thirty until five. I thought you should know."

Lukowski and MacNab looked at each other. It sounded like the uncle had a solid alibi. Bateman had been due home at five to dress for his testimonial dinner.

"Let me get this straight," said Lukowski. "Mr. Sweeney was with you from nine-thirty until five on Saturday the twelfth?"

"That's right. He didn't want to take the workshop, but I insisted. He's had a lot of bounced checks, and I let him know that if he wished to continue to bank with us he'd have to show he was willing to learn how to handle his cash flow better."

"A lot of these little merchants aren't cooperative,"

said Mr. LaRue. "We have to make it clear to them how much they'd benefit from some skill-sharpening in the financial area."

"Tell me about the workshop," said Lukowski. "What was involved, actually?"

"It's really a wonderful program," said Ms. Olson eagerly. "It's at the Airport Hilton, a very nice facility, and we start with a continental breakfast, you know, coffee and sweet rolls, and we have panels and helpful handouts and things. And then there's lunch and a speaker. In the afternoon we break into small groups and talk about cash flow strategy and money mindsets." The policemen didn't ask for a definition of that term. "We had about fifteen participants."

"I see. And you are absolutely sure Mr. Sweeney was there all day?"

"I remember him well," said Ms. Olson. "He was disruptive and unpleasant."

"Yeah?" MacNab looked amused.

Ms. Olson pursed her lips. "He really was rather awful. Told everyone at his table in a loud voice that we'd forced him to attend. Of course we did no such thing. We simply made it clear to him that if he wished to continue to do business with us, he'd have to show good faith and an intention to behave more responsibly."

"I heard he ate four sweet rolls," snorted Mr. LaRue. "Told everyone he wanted to get his money's worth."

"You mean he had to pay to go to this thing?" said MacNab.

"Of course. The workshop cost two hundred dollars." Mr. LaRue smiled. "We make it easier, though. We take it right out of their accounts. An automatic transfer. We do everything we can to help the small business person."

"Is there any way Mr. Sweeney could have slipped out? At lunch, maybe," persisted Lukowski.

Ms. Olson shook her head. "No. I kept wishing he would. He sat next to me at lunch and complained about the food. Which was really very good. Chicken stroganoff."

"Maybe he slipped out early," said Lukowski, thinking it more likely than not, considering the man's attitude.

"I saw him get into his car in the parking lot at five," said Ms. Olson. "He made some unpleasant remarks about his cash flow being actually hurt by the workshop. 'I should've been wrenching,' he said. Really, he missed the whole point. He couldn't take a long-term view of his business."

"Well, thank you for coming forward," said MacNab. "This may be very important."

"She won't have to testify in court, will she?" said Mr. LaRue.

"Maybe. We'll let you know." MacNab rose.

"I'll have to check with my area manager. They may not want us to become involved," said the manager.

"Don't be ridiculous," said MacNab testily. "Your area manager doesn't have jurisdiction over the police and the courts."

He gave Lukowski a look, rolling his eyes toward the ceiling.

Lukowski gave him a sympathetic twinkle and gave the two bankers a nice smile. It never failed. A lot of civilians were nervous wrecks when it came to court. He sometimes wondered if they didn't somehow feel guilty about their own lives, and that they might be arrested and whisked away if they participated in the judicial process. It was also typical of them to think their boss had more clout than the police. It was a wonder, thought Lukowski, that anything got taken care of, what with all the wimps in the world afraid of getting involved.

"Well," said MacNab as they left the bank, "that eliminates the uncle, as far as I can see. The hotel is way down by the airport. He never could have sneaked out and killed Bateman without being missed. Old Cosmo is off the hook."

"Looks like the nephew's left holding the bag," agreed Lukowski. "The grocery bag."

"As far as I can tell," said MacNab, "all we need now is a confession. Or some physical evidence connecting Carstairs to the crime. Otherwise, the best we can hope for is that Carstairs tries to cover things up and gets himself in deeper."

Lukowski snapped his fingers. "Hey, I forgot to tell you, there was one more thing the junkman said."

"Yeah? What?"

"He already told Carstairs about those groceries in the dumpster. I notice Carstairs didn't tell us himself."

"Are you surprised?" said MacNab. "Face it, the guy's guilty as hell."

The two men returned to their office to discover a stack of telephone messages. "Hey," said Lukowski, "here's one from Carstairs."

"Good," said MacNab. "Maybe he can't take it any more, he's going to confess and get it over with and I can go on that vacation."

"Why don't you take a listen," said Lukowski, punching up the number and switching on the phone's conference feature.

"Oh, thank you for returning my call," said Charles stiffly. "I've been giving it some thought, and there are a few things I should probably tell you about the case."

"Oh really," said Lukowski, raising an eyebrow in the direction of MacNab.

"Well we've stumbled onto a few things around here I thought you should know about." Charles explained about the cocaine dealings at Hi-Tech Auto, and about his encounter with the sct-back man. MacNab rolled his eyes and muttered, "The man of a thousand leads." Charles was concluding now, " . . . and I thought that if Bateman happened on some of these illegal activities he might have been murdered." He cleared his throat nervously to fill in a pause Lukowski had purposely left in the conversation. "You know maybe that lesbian who details cars killed him," he added. "Bateman was really sexist. I can imagine he might say something to set her off. Of course only Uncle Cosmo would know if she was due there that Saturday."

"Okay," summarized Lukowski, "you're saying we should check out the Hi-Tech people, the guy with the shotgun you describe, and the auto detailer who knew about the key?" MacNab rolled his eyes and said, "Jesus," softly.

"Well yes," said Charles. "And there's more. I had a talk with that private detective—Ferguson. He told me why he was staking the place out." Charles summarized Ferguson's story. "I really think there's something fishy about that Fast Eddie character," he said. "And I think we should find out who was in that tow truck up at the wrecking yard on the night of the day Bateman was murdered."

Lukowski noted the *we*. Carstairs was beginning to think he was a cop. "Well, that's all real interesting," he said. "We'll look into some of this. Thanks for calling."

He hung up. "Well, what do you think?"

"I think the guy's blaming everyone in the world," said MacNab. "The more suspects he comes up with the more sure I get he's our guy. The one about the dyke is the worst." He shook his head. "Pathetic. Notice we didn't hear a word about the steak in the dumpster?"

"Still, we'd better check out that business at the wrecking yard," said Lukowski. "Find out what Ferguson saw."

"You're right," said MacNab, sighing. "That Ferguson is the biggest flake in the world. Makes this Carstairs look legit."

At his end, Charles hung up the phone and smiled. He felt better about having told the police what he knew. Surely they'd appreciate his frankness. Of course, he'd omitted the detail of the groceries in the dumpster. It would be just as well if the murder couldn't be traced to the shop. But the set-back man and the wrecking yard, well, he'd held back on that because of Uncle Cosmo. But the longer Uncle Cosmo remained missing, the less interest Charles had in protecting his reputation. He was beginning to resent him highly for having dumped all these problems on him. Charles felt good about having given the police so much good information. Maybe they'd stop suspecting him.

CHAPTER
14

CHARLES had hoped he wouldn't have to work Saturdays. Uncle Cosmo, he recalled, usually had to, even though he swore he wouldn't. Jobs wouldn't get out on Friday afternoons, so Uncle Cosmo would come in on Saturdays and try to finish up. Charles always wondered why he didn't just put off the customers until Monday. Now that he was in charge, he knew. Uncle Cosmo had been trying to generate some extra cash to put in the bank and cover all the checks he wrote that week.

If Charles hadn't figured it out, Sylvia would have told him. She even booked a few jobs for Saturday and impressed upon him the need to collect a couple of hundred more to make the payroll on Monday. He was here all alone, of course. The mechanics weren't around, and Sylvia wasn't there either. Charles manfully struggled to juggle the phones (which kept ringing because all the regular customers seemed to know the place was unofficially open on Saturdays) and to finish up Friday's jobs.

First, he felt sorry for himself. But after he'd started

working and learned how much more he could accomplish when he wasn't supervising anyone, he actually began to enjoy it.

Presently he heard the front door open and went into the office. There he beheld two people, one at either end of a huge transmission encrusted with grease.

A middle-aged man in a baseball cap held up one end. At the other was a woman about the same age, presumably his wife, who groaned and let her end fall to the carpet with a clunk and a gush of transmission fluid from the rear seal.

"Can I help you?" he asked, rather nonplussed.

"You bet you can," said the man irritably. "I've spoken to you people about this transmission job you did for me. It's no damn good."

"You shouldn't have brought it in like that," Charles said. The woman sank onto the green plastic sofa, exhausted.

"We couldn't afford to have the car towed across Puget Sound on the Bremerton ferry," said the man. "So the wife and I just threw it in the back of my pickup."

"If you'd taken the torque converter off it wouldn't have been so heavy," said Charles, wondering if he should bring the woman a glass of water or something.

"Never mind that," said the man. "Are you going to make good on the rebuild job you did?"

"I've only been here about a week," said Charles. "Have you got the invoice? Let's see if we can reconstruct what happened."

"It's no use," said the woman weakly. "He won't do a damned thing. They're all crooks."

Charles was annoyed because he'd tried to be pleasant about the whole thing. "Look," he said firmly. "I'll be glad to discuss this with you, but I need to know what was done.''

"Cost me twelve hundred damn dollars. I should've gone to AAMCO.'' The man lowered his end of the transmission to the floor.

Charles wondered whether the transmission had really been that much of a basket case or whether he was seeing one of Cosmo's wall-jobs. He also wondered how he could get himself a twelve-hundred-dollar job, and soon.

"Let's see that invoice,'' he said.

"Here,'' said the man, producing a flimsy piece of pink paper, and waving it triumphantly at Charles. "And don't try anything funny. I have a Xerox of it.''

"In your lawyer's safe, I presume,'' said Charles sarcastically. He scrutinized the bill, making a mental note to check that the transmission was indeed the transmission that Cosmo had worked on before he promised any work.

"And if you don't take care of me right, I'm going to the Better Business Bureau, and writing that troubleshooter lady in the *Seattle Times*.''

"Just settle down,'' said Charles rather heatedly. The invoice indicated the transmission had been totally rebuilt. There was also a guarantee. Six months. If it hadn't been for Uncle Cosmo's confidently scrawled guarantee, Charles would never have looked at the date of the invoice. He was startled to see the work had been done three years previously.

"We did this three years ago,'' he said.

"So?'' The man made his hands into fists and advanced.

"Get this transmission out of here,'' said Charles. "How dare you come in here and impugn my integrity.''

"Oh, my God,'' said the woman. "I can't stand it. I can't carry that damn thing any more.''

151

"All right, all right," said Charles, shoving her aside as she took her place at the end of the transmission. "Step aside. I'll help you."

Twenty minutes later, the man nagging and complaining the whole time, Charles had managed to get the transmission back in the pickup and the couple on its way.

Exhausted, he went back into the office. The phone rang. It was Sylvia Snow.

"I've been worrying about you," she said. "Are you writing up any bills?"

"If I get any of these jobs done I will."

"I still haven't told you the correct procedure. That sales tax is off."

"I'll do what I can and you can fix it on Monday."

"I took home some of the books," she said. "I thought you might want to talk about them. The results of my survey of staff productivity are very instructive."

"I'm sure they are. But I need to get some of these cars out. The customers are complaining. I'll be lucky to finish by five, grab a pizza, and collapse."

"I've noticed you eat a lot of junk food," said Sylvia.

"Yeah. So?"

"Why don't you come by my place? I'll make you a decent meal, and then we can go over the books."

Charles had received many similar invitations. The mere mention of his junk food habits seemed to inspire young women to invite him to dinner. Usually he squirmed. Now he was pleased. He accepted, and as he wrenched away in the empty shop he wondered about Sylvia Snow. He wondered what her apartment was like and what kind of cook she was. He wondered whether she would charge him overtime for going over the books on Saturday night.

Charles, a good-looking young man in what was, demographically speaking, a buyer's market, seldom brought wine or flowers to his hostesses. Something about Miss Snow, her rather formal manner and her brusque ability with the books, inspired him to do something. Before he left his apartment, after a quick, degreasing shower, he rummaged in his freezer compartment and came up with a frozen cheesecake. It was the last uneaten part of his alibi weekend, the orgy of junk food in which he'd indulged while moping over losing tenure.

Sylvia Snow's building was not as he imagined it. A grim-looking bunkerlike edifice, relieved only by unimaginative use of concrete patio block and wrought iron balconies overlooking the freeway, it reminded him of his graduate school days.

Once inside her apartment, however, he could see the signs of her aggressively ethnic taste. Over the olive drab shag carpeting were Turkish kilims. There was a shelf with pre-Columbian pottery—museum replicas, he assumed. On the walls were a framed poster of Nijinksy in full leap and a Japanese print of a cat. Sylvia Snow herself was decked out in what might have been an Afghan dress and peculiar pointed felt shoes with bells on them. Her hair, freed from its balletic chignon, hung in dark waves around her face.

"Did you get that carb job squared away?" she asked earnestly at the door.

"Yes. And they paid up. Put it on Visa."

"I've been meaning to talk to you about that," she said. "You should charge extra for credit cards. The bank charges you, you know."

She ushered him in and consulted her watch. Charles thought the watch an odd touch with the Afghan dress and the harem shoes. "Do you mind terribly if we watch the six o'clock news?" she said. "There might be something about, you know, the murder." She seemed a little apologetic. "I've been watching the news every night."

She switched on an ancient television set that seemed to be made of Bakelite plastic. Charles watched the lead stories about arms control talks and Princess Diana, while Sylvia disappeared into the kitchen. She returned in a moment with some ammoniated white curdish cheese and a carafe of red wine. The wine tasted rough and gritty.

"And in local news," said a cheerful blond, "there are new developments in the Bateman murder case. Seattle police have found the late Dr. Bateman's car in an airport parking lot." Charles and Sylvia watched footage of a Volkswagen Rabbit being towed out of a parking lot. "As you recall," continued the blond, in a perky voice-over, "University of Washington professor Roland Bateman was found dead in the back of an old Volvo at Cosmo's Car Center, a north end auto shop. Today his own car was found at the airport. Police lab findings indicate that, interestingly, as the professor had indicated to colleagues he meant to visit the auto shop to complain about a tuneup, tests show that he had reason to complain. Spark plugs and points, allegedly replaced, were old and worn, and the engine idled roughly."

"Terrific," moaned Charles. "Now the whole town knows about Uncle Cosmo's wall-jobs."

"Wall-jobs?" said Sylvia. "Sounds obscene."

"It means you park the car against the shop wall, don't do anything to it, and charge the customer when he comes back."

"That's terrible," said Sylvia, offering him a plate of crinkly crackers with sesame seeds. "But it does give you a profit margin of a hundred percent on the job."

Now they saw footage of the front of Cosmo's Car

Center. You couldn't tell from the pictures when the camera crew had shot them, but there was something interesting on the side of the frame. Two figures were clearly visible. One of them was opening his wallet and giving money to the other. The man handing over the cash was Fast Eddie, unmistakable in his tractor cap and greasy hair. The man on the receiving end was Phil.

The blond's face reappeared. "In a related story, our consumer reporter has some tips on how to choose your auto repair shop. It's a jungle out there, right Madge?"

Madge, a sincere-looking black woman, nodded. "That's right, Gloria. A little knowledge can save you big bucks when it's time to have any automotive work done."

Gloria came back on the screen. "But first, it's time for those lottery results. Got your tickets ready? Here are this week's winning numbers."

Sylvia went to the set and switched it off.

"Did you see what I saw?" said Charles.

"It looked like Phil was collecting some cash from our wrecking yard friend," said Sylvia. "I wonder why?"

"Maybe because he did some moonlighting for him."

Sylvia looked thoughtful. "Or maybe there's a more sinister reason. That Fast Eddie acted awfully nervous out at the wrecking yard. Maybe he's paying off Phil because Phil knows something."

"About the murder?"

"Why not?"

Charles sipped his wine. "Phil could use some extra money, I guess. Steve said he was heavily into hock with the Rench-Rite rep. Maybe I should let him moonlight."

"If Phil knows something that can get those detectives off your back, I'd think you'd like to hear about it," said Sylvia, her dark eyes flashing.

"Even if Fast Eddie is guilty about something it doesn't have to have anything to do with Bateman. There's plenty of sleazy stuff happening around that shop. And, according to that private eye, around Elwood's Wrecking Yard."

"What sleazy stuff?" Sylvia asked. "Besides the occasional wall-job?"

Charles filled her in on the set-back man and on the cocaine business that seemed to be operating out of Hi-Tech Auto down the alley.

"Wow," she said, refilling their glasses. The wine tasted a little better after you got used to it. "This opens up all kinds of possibilities."

"Like what?" Charles sensed that Sylvia thought he was a little dense and felt that Charles lacked the proper level of enthusiasm for figuring out who killed Bateman.

"Maybe Bateman wandered into the shop that Saturday and came across some illegal activity," she said.

"I already suggested that to the police," he replied. "I've told them practically everything I've learned, and they haven't figured out a thing."

"What do you mean *practically* everything," she said sharply.

Maybe it was the wine, maybe it was her sharp tone. Charles heard himself telling Sylvia Snow about the groceries in the dumpster.

Sylvia frowned. "So he was there. But the Volvo wasn't. And then it was, later, with him welded in it."

"I wish the police would find out who did it," said Charles.

"They think you did it," she said. "I'm sure of it."

"Maybe that MacNab does," said Charles, "but I'm sure Lukowski knows I'm innocent."

"They're probably concentrating on proving you did it

156

rather than on looking for anyone else. I know how they think. I used to go out with a cop in New York.''

Charles found himself surprised and irritated that Sylvia Snow had had any men in her life.

"Of course," she added, "he wasn't in homicide. He was in vice.''

"I've given the police plenty of good leads," complained Charles. "I don't think they've checked out the department at the university thoroughly enough." He told her about Smathers, Gunderson, the intense Eleanor Zimmer, and Larry de la Roque.

"I bet it's easy to sneak out of a mental hospital." Sylvia became very animated. "He's got himself a perfect alibi. We just have to break it.''

"How do we do that?"

"It sounds like the guy is already a little over the edge. I bet if you just acted chummy with him, he might tell you all about it.''

"Not very likely," said Charles. "Besides, he acted like *I'd* done it.''

"Well, it bears looking into," said Sylvia with an impatient frown. "When are you going to be on campus next?''

Charles sighed. "I hate going there. It's very uncomfortable." He followed her into the kitchen, where she served up plates with some sort of Algerian-looking couscous arrangement with a side of eggplant. It looked dreadful, and Charles polished off his glass of wine hastily, as if to numb his senses for the ordeal. Didn't anyone know how to make a nice pot roast anymore? Charles's mother had made an excellent pot roast. He was not fond of the cuisine of the Third World.

Over dinner, which tasted better than it looked, Charles found himself pouring out his troubles with the department

157

and Dr. Bateman. "It's been hell," he concluded. "I've been in school all my life. I liked being a professor. I always felt sorry for anyone who wasn't."

"You can't love any career that much," said Sylvia firmly. "You just set yourself up to get kicked in the teeth." She sounded bitter.

"Why can't I just do what I want to do?" he said, hoping he wasn't whining. He had expected her to be more sympathetic.

"Because there's no justice in the world, and you have to be flexible and make your own way, and develop an identity for yourself beyond your work."

"You seem awfully sure about it," said Charles. "Don't you care about accounting?"

"It's a means to an end. I'm not going to let myself be defined by what I do."

"That's easy for you to say," said Charles. "Being a scholar is a special calling. Besides, you haven't had the rug pulled out from under you like I have."

"Yes, I have," she said, rather angrily, he thought, holding up her head at a firm angle, her chin pointing forward, her eyes intense. "And I put a lot more years into it than you did. And my whole body and soul too.

"Dancers start young. I spent every hour after school at class. I gave up social life. I got a spotty education. I danced on injuries, I starved myself, I watched my friends fail and hurt themselves and turn anorectic.

"I was Clara in *Nutcracker*, and when I was bigger, I made it to New York and a job in the corps. They told me how to wear my hair, and not to get a tan. They told me I wasn't working hard enough, that I didn't care enough, and that a thousand other girls would kill to get my job. They were right about that. I lived in cheap apartments and danced my little heart out. I was a living sacrifice to art. Pale, thin, and hurting.''

"What happened. Why aren't you still dancing?''

"Because I'm not stupid,'' said Sylvia. "I figured that I'd spent half my childhood and all of my adolescence hurting and depriving myself. I wasn't going to make it out of the corps, and I'd seen what happened to the girls who got too old. Most of them hadn't even finished high school. They didn't have time. Some of them taught. I wasn't prepared to start torturing a whole new crop of little girls and humoring the ballet mothers. It's child abuse.

"I got myself a job working in the company's accounting department while I still had my youth and my health and my dignity. Everyone thought it was so pathetic that I'd stopped dancing. To them, it's the only thing in the world. Just the way you probably feel about being a professor. But there are lots of things to do in the world. Maybe not so glamorous, but not so masochistic, either. It turned out I had a knack for it. And people treated me better. Like a person.''

"Do you miss dancing?'' said Charles, fascinated.

"Sure I do. But it wasn't any kind of a life.''

"Well I'm sure I can get a job in my field somewhere,'' said Charles. "I can't bear the thought of starting over again, but maybe I'll have to.''

Sylvia carried away the plates. She cut Charles's offering, the frozen cheesecake, thawed now, and made coffee.

"I usually don't tell people about my dancing,'' she said. "They don't understand. They think I failed somehow when I quit.''

They went back into the living room. Charles was trying subtly to check out Sylvia's body beneath the shapeless afghan garment. Did she have a lithe dancer's body under

159

there, with long, well-shaped legs, the kind of small, high breasts described in cheap novels as "pert," and a boyish, well-muscled bottom?

She leaned over the table, pushing the dessert things to one side. He felt a little frisson at her closeness. Maybe this evening would end as so many similar evenings had, with his concerned hostess taking it upon herself to minister not only to his needs for a wholesome, non-junk-food meal.

"You don't mind if we start right away, do you?" she said, slamming the heavy ledgers down on the coffee table. "We can drink our coffee at the same time." She consulted her watch. "I won't charge you," she added. "But I'll just keep track of this so I can take comp time if we ever have a slow period."

CHAPTER
15

CHARLES slept in a little on Monday morning. He felt guilty about it, but not as guilty as he might have if a class full of eager freshmen were waiting for him. He consoled himself with the thought that Sylvia could handle anything for a half hour or so, as he hit the snooze-bar on the clock radio one more time.

It just seemed all so overwhelming. The business teetering on the brink, the police so sure he was a murderer, Uncle Cosmo apparently vanished from the face of the earth, not to mention the fact that he hadn't even started putting his resumé and application letters together. What made it extra hard to get up was the fact that a heavy Seattle rain was falling. Through a supreme effort of will, Charles turned off his electric blanket. After it had cooled down, he was able to summon up the courage to get out of bed.

When he arrived at the shop, at around a quarter of ten, he was alarmed to see Mrs. Scroggins from across the alley leaning on the counter and having an intense discussion with Sylvia. Mrs. Scroggins wore her usual print housedress and apron, weatherized with a see-through plastic raincoat and bonnet. The scuffs on her feet were encased in clear galoshes. What did *she* want? Charles had tried very hard not to run afoul of her. He gave both women a perfunctory nod and barreled past them into the shop area to escape.

"Goddamnit!" Steve bellowed. He was staring at the cold tank, a thirty gallon drum filled with solvent and topped with a plastic housing, valve, and safety lock. The tank was used to clean carburetors and other delicate parts. Charles wondered which would be worse, listening to Mrs. Scroggins's complaints, or Steve's. He took a chance on Steve. "What's the matter now?" he said.

"I just dropped the keys to this car I'm working on in there," said Steve. Charles was pleased Steve had made a mistake for a change, instead of pointing out someone else's. "It would never have happened if this shop were clean. I slipped on some of that spilled crank-case oil, fell against this damn thing, and the keys flew out of my hand."

Charles sighed. He handed Steve a pair of heavy elbow-length rubber gloves nearby. "Go ahead, fish them out," he said.

The intercom crackled. Sylvia's voice said, "Charles, could you come into the office for a moment please?"

Charles sighed again. What was Mrs. Scroggins going to complain about now? And what city inspector would she unleash on him? He worried she'd call the fire department. He hadn't had time to check it out, but there seemed to be a lot of extension cords looped around the walls from cup hooks, and he wasn't sure the fire extinguisher worked.

"You've met Mrs. Scroggins, I gather," said Sylvia.

Charles nodded. "She's concerned about the parking situation in the alley."

"I understand this is a long-standing problem," began Charles. "I've tried to make sure we never leave any cars blocking the alley for more than a minute or so. Sometimes, when we're bringing them around to the back of the shop we have to—"

"Oh, save it for the law," said Mrs. Scroggins. "I got a complete record of all your comings and goings. I know you're up to no good here, and I intend to make sure you don't get away with a damn thing." She began to wave a spiral-bound notebook at them.

Sylvia's eyes widened. "Let me see that," she said, snatching the book away. Mrs. Scroggins didn't seem annoyed that her book had been unceremoniously grabbed from her. She stood there looking smug while they examined the pages. Charles looked over Sylvia's shoulder. It seemed that Mrs. Scroggins had made daily entries of the transgressions of Cosmo's Car Center and its employees. Mostly they were times and license numbers of cars blocking the alley, but some indicated comings and goings. "Tough-looking customer arrives 9:00 P.M., dealer plates," read one that Charles assumed referred to the set-back man.

Sylvia was flipping pages until she reached Saturday the twelfth, when Dr. Bateman had disappeared. There was no entry. Mrs. Scroggins gave them a beady eye and seemed to know what they were doing. "That's right. I was visiting my daughter that weekend, or I would have known who killed that poor man. You people are lucky I was away."

"Look at this," said Sylvia. She pointed at an entry for Thursday the seventeenth. "Young guy with greasy long

hair and a baseball cap double-parks Volvo, 11:00 P.M.,"
it read. The license number followed.

"Is that the same car?" said Sylvia, turning to Charles.

"I think so. I think the license number is the same,"
said Charles.

"Sound like anyone you know at the wheel?" said
Sylvia.

"It sure does." Charles looked grim.

"What are you people talking about," snapped Mrs.
Scroggins.

"I think we'd better call the police," said Charles.

Sylvia nodded. "Detective MacNab gave me his private
extension," she said. "I'll call him directly."

"Mrs. Scroggins," said Charles, "you may have some
important evidence here in this book."

"You bet I do," she said. She made a motion as if to
grab it back. "I bet you'd like to make sure the cops never
see it. Why, some of these infractions go back years, not
to mention all the dope that hophead's been smoking in
that alley."

"Please give me the book," said Charles. "I want the
police to see it." He began to grind his teeth.

"No way," she exclaimed, grabbing it out of his hand.
"I know what you're up to, with your sneaky ways. You
may have got a good education, but you're cut from the
same cloth as that old crook Cosmo. You're going to
destroy the evidence."

Sylvia put down the phone. "MacNab and Lukowski
are out," she said. "I left a message."

"She won't give it to me," said Charles to Sylvia.

Sylvia paused for a moment, taking in the scene. Then
she said, "Don't do it Mrs. Scroggins, don't do it. Hand it
right over to the police. I've called two detectives, and

164

when they call back we'll give it right to them. It's very important they see it. I think you've got some real grievances here.'' Sylvia gave Charles a meaningful look.

"Atta girl," said Mrs. Scroggins. "I'm glad someone around here cares about right and wrong."

"I won't let Mr. Carstairs take it away from you," continued Sylvia. "Just sit right there until the police come."

Charles wasn't sure it was really necessary to humor the old girl, but it seemed to have worked. And her evidence could be vital. Sylvia was settling Mrs. Scroggins in on the couch and making her a cup of coffee.

Charles went back into the shop, terribly excited. Here's exactly what they needed. Proof that the Volvo hadn't been at the shop. That someone brought it, containing the body, to the shop, where it had been discovered the next day. And that someone certainly sounded like Fast Eddie. But why had Fast Eddie killed Dr. Bateman? And welded him into the trunk? And left him at Cosmo's? It was all too bizarre.

"Take a look at this," said Steve, coming over to him with his long rubber glove on. "Look what I found in the cold tank."

"The keys, I hope," said Charles. He had already had to get a locksmith out to make a new set of customers' keys that Bud had lost.

"No, this," said Steve. He held up a huge wrench. "Now what the hell's this doing in the cold tank? Let's face it, this is a poorly run shop. I've been looking for this son-of-a-bitch for a week or more."

Charles stared in fascination at the wrench. It was perfectly clean, but then it would be after a week or more in that solvent. Any traces of blood and hair would be eaten away by chemicals. And if Steve hadn't been feeling around in there, the tank would have been removed by the chemical company and, under strict federal regulations, disposed of in some chemical waste dump.

Charles was confused. He had just learned that Fast Eddie had delivered that car, presumably with a body in it. Now it looked like a weapon had been disposed of on the premises. And Bateman's groceries had been in the dumpster, too. Of course, the wrench could be a coincidence, but he doubted it. To get a wrench in that drum you had to open it up, releasing a safety lock.

He went into the office to tell Sylvia what Steve had found. She stood there, handing him the telephone receiver. "It's your Uncle Cosmo," she said. "Calling collect from Anchorage, Alaska."

CHAPTER
16

"**U**NCLE Cosmo," exclaimed Charles. "Just the man I want to talk to!"

"Hi," said Uncle Cosmo. "Sorry about calling collect, but I'm out of change." The voice was unmistakable. "What the hell's going on down there? I took a plane from Vegas up to Alaska and there was a Seattle paper on the plane. Apparently the cops found some car at the airport and someone was killed at your shop. What the hell's going on down there?"

"You've got to get back here," said Charles. "You'll never believe what's been happening."

"Forget it," said Cosmo jovially. "I quit that business and I mean to stay quit. I'm sure you can handle everything just fine. But I had to call and see what's going on at the shop."

"The police have been looking for you. Where were you?"

"You know we had that trouble with your aunt's birth certificate—"

"I know, I got the postcard."

"So we went to Vegas for a while, but it was kind of dull. Gambling's lost its appeal now that I'm rich." He chuckled contentedly.

"What are you doing in Alaska?" said Charles.

"It's going to take ten more days for that passport to get processed, so your aunt checked into one of those beauty farms in California. Cost a pile, let me tell you, but she wanted to look good on the beach in the Bahamas. So I figured I'd get in some fishing up here. I've always wanted to go fishing in Alaska."

"Listen," said Charles, "let me tell you all about it." It took a while, but Charles managed to tell Uncle Cosmo all of it. Mrs. Scroggins, sipping coffee suspiciously on the couch, listened eagerly to his side of the conversation. Sylvia hovered nervously around.

Charles told about the discovery of the body, about the police being around, about Fast Eddie having been seen driving the Volvo in question to the shop. He left out a few details. There was no need to tell his uncle about the set-back man, or that Charles had told the police about him. He didn't want to sound like a snitch. And he thought he'd better avoid any mention of that wrench, too, and the groceries the junkman had found in the dumpster and told him about. After all, he wanted the police to pursue Fast Eddie, and get off the idea that the murder had taken place in the shop. One word of the wrench or the jettisoned groceries and Mrs. Scroggins would be writing it down in her little book and blabbing to the cops. Charles was mindful of what Sylvia Snow had said on Saturday night. The police, she felt, weren't as interested in solving the case as in proving their case against Charles. Why give them anything that brought the crime closer to his doorstep?

Finally he stopped for breath. "So you've got to come back here and tell the police what went on here that Saturday," said Charles. "Were you expecting Bateman?"

"I wasn't expecting anyone," said Uncle Cosmo. "I had to go to some damn seminar the bank put on. I told Bateman I wouldn't be in on Saturday, but he seemed to think I was lying. He said he'd come anyway and wait for me. You know, I think that guy was the worst pain-in-the-neck customer I ever had."

"I can imagine that," said Charles. "But believe me, he's been a worse pain in the neck dead. What did go on here that Saturday? The mechanics say they weren't around."

"I don't know what went on there that day. Phil was going to come in and work on his own car, I think. I don't know."

"Well, are you coming back down to tell the police what you know?" said Charles.

"Aw hell, they'll just hassle me and screw up things some more. This passport thing is bad enough. I'll never get to hit that beach. I don't need any more aggravation. I thought I'd be free of aggravation when I was rich."

"You don't know the meaning of the word," snapped Charles. "Why, they've been all over this place. Took away all the tools looking for a wrench to match the crease in Bateman's skull. Threw up a police line around the place. Drove away customers. And if that isn't enough, I seem to be their chief suspect!"

"They took away all the tools," said Uncle Cosmo. "Gee."

"Uncle Cosmo, they suspect *me*," said Charles.

"Why should they?" said Uncle Cosmo.

"Bateman's the guy that—"

"Fired you?" said Cosmo.

"I wasn't fired. I just didn't get tenure."

"I don't see how my coming down there is going to help you," said Cosmo. "I was at the bank thing all day. I don't know what happened. Maybe you *did* come in and kill the guy."

"Thanks a lot," said Charles.

"I don't think you did it, but I can't come up with anything that proves you didn't, can I?" said Uncle Cosmo. "Anyway, from what you tell me, there's nothing that proves he was killed at the shop. Not if Eddie brought the car to the shop. That old lady Scroggins will be useful for the first time in her life. How is the old bitch?"

"But the car *was* your car. It was parked in the alley once. How can you be so calm about this?" demanded Charles. "A guy was found dead in your shop. The police think I did it."

Cosmo sighed. "All I want to do is go to the Bahamas. Listen, you hold everything together. If they really think you did it, well, I'll be glad to help you out with a lawyer or whatever."

"Where are you staying up in Anchorage?" said Charles. "Maybe the police can just talk to you over the phone."

Cosmo named a hotel. "But I'm heading back into the bush for a few days. There's some mighty good fishing up this way. I got myself a guide, and I'm all ready to go. I'll be back in a week. Tell 'em that.

"I know this is a tough break, kid," he added. "But I'm sure it'll all work out."

"Aren't you even curious about this?" Charles asked. "Don't you wonder who did it?"

"Could have been anyone, I guess," said Uncle Cosmo.

"This crime thing's getting out of hand. There're a lot of disturbed people in the world."

Uncle Cosmo hung up before Charles could say anything else.

"Well?" said Sylvia. "Well?"

Charles took her out into the shop area to tell her what he had learned. He didn't particularly want Mrs. Scroggins listening to every word and putting it down in her notebook. Bud and Phil were out moving cars, and Steve was in a world of his own, cursing softly into an engine compartment.

"I guess you heard my end of it." He explained Uncle Cosmo's travel itinerary. "He sounds like he doesn't want to get involved," concluded Charles, "but I'll tell the police where he's staying."

Sylvia listened carefully, asking a few questions here and there. "He claims he was at the bank all day when Bateman disappeared," she said, thoughtfully.

"Yes. I told you he couldn't kill anyone," said Charles. "Have you been suspecting him all along?"

"To tell the truth, I had," she said. "But I never could come up with a motive, or any reason your uncle would just leave the body here. Now it looks as though Fast Eddie dumped it here."

"Listen, Sylvia," he said in a whisper, "something else has come up. Steve just found a big two-inch combination wrench in that drum over there. I think it might have been the weapon. I didn't want to tell the police," he added guiltily. "I don't want them to tie the crime in with this place—and, by association, me. But I can't figure it. What would a weapon be doing here if he wasn't killed here?"

Sylvia shrugged. "Maybe Fast Eddie dumped the body *and* the weapon here," she said.

171

Charles thought about that for a second. "But Steve seemed to recognize the tool. He said it had been missing."

"One wrench is just like another, isn't it?" said Sylvia.

This wasn't strictly true, but Charles didn't have a chance to explain that mechanics recognized individual tools from the variety of nicks and scratches they developed over years of use because the phone rang.

Sylvia went in to answer it and handed the phone to Charles. A sobbing woman was at the other end. "And you worked on the car just yesterday. I wanted it running perfectly so I could make this bid opening. And now I'm stranded. You've got to come and help me."

Charles didn't want to leave before the police came. "Well, can't you have it towed?" he asked. "I'll reimburse you for the towing and a cab."

"You have to come get me," said the woman. "I'm nowhere near anything. It'd take ages for a tow truck to get here. And there aren't any cabs—"

"Where are you?" said Charles. "I've got a map of the city here."

"You'll need a state map," she said. "I'm halfway to Olympia. Somewhere between Tacoma and Olympia."

Charles calculated the cost of a tow truck halfway to the state capitol. "What's the problem with the car exactly?" he said.

"It's broken," sobbed the woman. "That's what's the matter with it. It just won't run."

Charles guided her through the motions of changing fuses. Fuses didn't seem to be the problem.

"Listen," said the woman angrily, "this could cost me plenty. My company's been trying to get this state contract for years. Thousands are at stake. If I don't get there, I'll sue you for everything you've got. My lost business, and the towing, and the transportation, and my mental anguish. My husband's an attorney," she added.

"Okay," said Charles. "I'll get down there. How much time do you have?"

After some calculations, Charles figured he could get Mrs. Colman to the bid opening if he could fix the car in twenty minutes or so. Otherwise, he guessed, he'd have to drive her to Olympia in his tow truck.

He threw some tools and parts into the back of the tow truck, and instructed Sylvia to keep trying the police. "I'll call you when I can," he said, and headed out in the now blinding rain to the freeway.

CHAPTER
17

I T was some hours later that MacNab and Lukowski emerged from a tedious meeting outlining new procedures mandated by changes in state law regarding the presentation of physical evidence and went to get their phone messages.

"This is interesting," said Lukowski, after he'd spoken to Sylvia. "That arty-looking bookkeeper down at Cosmo's says she's got the evidence we need to crack the case. Seems that little old lady across the alley keeps a journal of the comings and goings at Cosmo's Car Center."

"We already talked to her," complained MacNab. "Hates their guts, but she wasn't around on that Saturday. Seemed like a head-case anyway."

"Well, Carstairs is presenting her as his star witness now," said Lukowski thoughtfully.

"I guess we better go down and check it out," said MacNab. "But I'm getting tired of chasing down his leads. That wrecking yard didn't pan out. All we found out is that Eddie kid has a record. Big deal. Probably gave Carstairs the idea of framing him."

"You know," said Lukowski, "I wonder if Carstairs has cooked up something funny with the old lady. You know, if she's crazy to begin with—"

"Yeah," said MacNab enthusiastically. "He's always trying to solve the damn case for us, any way but the way we see it. If we can show he's trying to fake up some evidence with this nutty old broad—"

"Let's see what she says." Lukowski was getting his topcoat.

Sylvia Snow looked animated and excited when they arrived. "She's still here," she said, indicating a small woman in a drab housedress and slippers, sitting on the couch next to a bundle of plastic, which appeared to be rain gear. "And there's more. Uncle Cosmo is found. He's in Alaska."

MacNab and Lukowski took down the name of the hotel.

"Aren't you excited we found him?" said Sylvia.

"We would have found him eventually," said MacNab. "Next time he tried to get the monthly check from his lottery winnings." He sensed this girl didn't have faith in the police. Probably madly in love with her boss. That sloppy-looking lady professor at the university had said women went for him big, and so did that weaselly Smathers. Mrs. Bateman had liked him well enough.

The two men turned their attention to Mrs. Scroggins. Mrs. Scroggins hauled out her notebook and, after asking to see their badges, came forth with a litany of complaints about the past and present management of Cosmo's Car Center, dating back to the day Cosmo had offered Mrs. Scroggins an insultingly small amount for the late Mr.

Scroggins's old Packard. "Thugs and crooks, all of them," she said. "Especially that smarmy nephew." Here at last, thought MacNab, was one woman who could see beyond flashy good looks.

It took a while, and Sylvia finally entered into the fray, but eventually the two detectives were presented with evidence that Mrs. Scroggins had seen the Volvo that had entombed Dr. Bateman's body.

"The tag's the same," said MacNab, consulting the license number in her notes.

"And we think," said Sylvia eagerly, "that the man behind the wheel was Fast Eddie. He works at Elwood's, a wrecking yard up in the north end. He's a very suspicious character."

"We'll check it out," said MacNab laconically, taking the notebook from Mrs. Scroggins and giving her a receipt for it.

"Now can you close these bums down, and give us some peace in that alley?" she demanded.

"We'll do what we can, ma'am," said Lukowski.

"If this is some kind of runaround I'll call the mayor's office," she said. "Thanks for the coffee, honey," she said to Sylvia. "It was real good what you did, not letting your boss destroy the evidence. I hope he doesn't fire you."

Lukowski and MacNab looked at each other. Whatever was going on in Mrs. Scroggins's head, it wasn't beyond the realm of possibility that she had been tricked somehow into providing this evidence. In any case, it was clear she was a shaky witness.

When they got back into the car MacNab said, "Well, do you want to go back out to that wrecking yard?"

"I was thinking we should get ahold of that Cosmo character," said Lukowski. "Interview him on the phone if we can or get a man in Anchorage to do it, or even get him down here as a material witness, against his will if we have to. Of course, he might want to cover for the nephew.''

"He can afford to," agreed MacNab. "His alibi's solid. Of course that means he can't provide his nephew with one." MacNab laughed. "Old Charles will just have to stick with Shirley Temple and Tarzan.''

CHAPTER
18

CHARLES found Mrs. Colman at a rest area about fifty miles south of Seattle. Her face was red and blotchy with the marks of recent tears, and she was accompanied by a surly-looking child of about three.

A quick investigation under the hood revealed that the problem was a simple one. Her accelerator linkage had become unattached. As she had had brake work done on the car last week, it was clear there was no connection between her present troubles and the work Cosmo's Car Center had done, but Charles knew that in the mind of the customer anything that happened to a car within a week of a visit to a garage was the shop's fault. Customers tended to believe that the new problem was either the result of poor workmanship or of deliberate sabotage to ensure more work. There were shops that did that sort of thing, but usually they were clever enough to fix things so that they gave out weeks or even months later.

It would have taken five minutes to reattach the accelerator linkage if it were all there. Unfortunately, a chunk

178

of it had fallen onto the freeway. Charles put the car on the hook, bundled Mrs. Colman and her child into the front of the tow truck, and headed south to Olympia.

Mrs. Colman, who had been ready to kill Charles when he arrived, now seemed mollified. Charles imagined it was some sort of Stockholm syndrome at work. The woman was entirely dependent on him to get her bid filed with the state. Mrs. Colman, it appeared, ran some vague sort of consulting firm from her rec room, and expected the state to pay her thousands of dollars for putting together a feasibility study. "I have a good chance," she explained. "They have to give women and minorities first consideration."

"Why don't they just let you mail the bid in?" said Charles, narrowly avoiding being sideswiped by a huge semi barreling down at him through the heavy rain.

"Oh, they do. But I didn't have the proposal ready, so I have to deliver it by hand," she explained. "It's been hard to get any work done lately because Elliott's been very cranky. He's sensitive. We think it's because he's gifted."

Charles ground his teeth. This woman had threatened to sue him for the business she might have lost, and she could have mailed the damn thing in in the first place. Besides, her car problems weren't his fault. He wondered what was going on back in Seattle. Had the police spoken to Mrs. Scroggins? Had they arrested Fast Eddie?

Elliott, squirming in Mrs. Colman's lap because there wasn't really room for him in the cab, spotted the golden arches of a McDonald's through the rain. He began to scream that he wanted a Happy Meal. Charles looked nervously over at the child. He was in a full-fledged tantrum now, kicking his feet in a staccato rhythm against the gearshift lever, which Charles tried to hold in place so they wouldn't all get killed on the freeway.

"Can't you get him settled down?" he said irritably.

"Elliott, why are you so angry?" said Mrs. Colman. "We want you to cooperate and stop crying."

"Mr. Rogers says it's okay to cry," screamed the child.

"After we deliver the bid," said Charles firmly, "I'll take you and Elliott to the bus station."

It was four o'clock by the time Charles made it back to the shop with Mrs. Colman's car. "Well?" he exclaimed, racing into the office. "What happened? Did the police come?"

"Yes," said Sylvia. "And they talked to Mrs. Scroggins and took her notebook away."

"Good. Now they can go shake the truth out of Fast Eddie."

Sylvia frowned. "I don't know, Charles. I'm kind of worried. Mrs. Scroggins may have seen Fast Eddie deliver that car here, but I don't know if she's really credible. I think those detectives thought she was nuts."

"Well, she is nuts," said Charles. "What difference does that make?"

"I just don't know how seriously they took her."

"They'd better get out and talk to Fast Eddie," said Charles. "And Uncle Cosmo too," he added. "You told them about him, I trust?"

"Of course." Sylvia looked a little embarrassed. "I hope you don't mind," she said, "but I had a little talk with Phil."

"What about?"

"Well, you told me your uncle said Phil was going to come in and work on his car that Saturday. He told us and the police that he didn't. So I told him they'd found Cosmo, and that Cosmo had said he'd planned to come in on Saturday."

"You asked him about it? Shouldn't the police have done that?"

"I couldn't help it. I wanted to see what he said."

"What *did* he say?"

"He said he had come in, for about an hour around ten, but he hadn't said so because he hadn't wanted to get involved. And that he wasn't sure he'd remembered to lock up, so he was afraid he'd get into trouble. I advised him to tell the police the truth."

"I doubt it makes too much difference," said Charles. "If he was in in the morning he wouldn't have seen anything. Bateman was alive and well until oneish, from what the papers say. Bill Gunderson saw him at school."

"I also told Phil about seeing him on the news. Taking that money from Eddie. You know, Phil's so high-strung, I didn't want to set him off or anything, but I had to know what he knew about Eddie," she said.

Charles looked nervously over his shoulder toward the direction of the shop area. "What did you get out of him?" he asked in a low voice.

She shrugged. "Just that Eddie had paid him off for the last moonlighting job. Apparently Eddie delivered the cars to be worked on nights, called Phil at work to discuss the repairs, and picked up the cars after work. He'd come by on his lunch hours to pay Phil. That's what he was doing when those TV cameras were taking pictures of Cosmo's Car Center."

"You think he's on the level?" said Charles.

"I guess so. I wish I knew what the police were up to."

"How are things going around here?" said Charles. "Made any money today?"

"As far as I know we're getting all the jobs out. We had a parts problem with that old Ford, though. Steve's been screaming all day about a windshield wiper motor. I've located a used one." She paused. "At Elwood's."

"Why don't I go up there and pick it up?" said Charles. "It might be interesting to find out if Eddie's still running around loose."

Her eyes shone. "That's just what I was thinking," she replied.

Charles got into his own car, an improvement over the tow truck, which had bald tires and excruciatingly slow and squeaky windshield wipers, and headed up to Elwood's.

The laconic Elwood at the counter seemed vague about a Ford of the right year and make, but suggested Charles go find Eddie and ask him about it. "He's out there under a car somewhere." Charles noticed that Elwood was flapping through a pile of pink slips—car registrations—no doubt belonging to the cars he planned to smash into cubes to make room for condominiums.

Charles picked his way through the lot. The rain came down harder than ever from a gunmetal gray sky. It wasn't like the soft rains he rather liked. All around him water cascaded from piles of old hulks. The ground beneath him was muddy.

He finally found Eddie, working beneath a car. At least he assumed it was Eddie. All he could see were a pair of thin legs in faded jeans and feet in scuffed black motorcycle boots sticking out from beneath a heavy old Buick. A greasy Seattle Mariner's baseball cap lay neatly at the side of the car.

"Eddie?" he said, but then he realized that Eddie wouldn't answer.

Eddie was under the car all right. Right under the car. Two jackstands lay on their sides on the ground. The car, missing its tires, lay directly on top of Eddie's chest.

Charles was reminded of the scene in *The Wizard of Oz* where the witch's feet appear from beneath Dorothy's house from Kansas. He stood there, paralyzed for a moment, before it occurred to him that there was a chance Eddie was alive. He had to go get help. He turned to run back to the office, but he'd only gone a couple of yards when he collided right into Detective MacNab. Lukowski was next to him. He felt their hands gripping his arms, and watched their faces staring down at the Buick and the pair of feet.

"Look at those marks in the mud," said MacNab. "By those jackstands." Charles could see grooves in the ground where the jackstands had been dragged or kicked away from the car.

"Where's One Hundred Forty-fifth Street?" asked Lukowski.

"A few blocks north," said MacNab, with satisfaction. "We're in the city limits. We've got jurisdiction."

Charles felt metal bands snapped around his wrists. "You're under arrest," said Lukowski.

CHAPTER
19

B Y seven o'clock, Lukowski and MacNab were exhausted. They'd sent out for more hamburgers and more coffee. Charles Carstairs had been given his rights at the wrecking yard, before the medics had arrived, before the scene had been thoroughly secured and gone over, before the jackstands were taken away in plastic bags and the photographs were taken, before the car had been lifted up to reveal the twisted form of Edward Earl Evans, a.k.a. Fast Eddie, wrench in hand, chest crushed.

But he hadn't wanted a lawyer just yet, although he made his one phone call to the woman who worked for him. Charles Carstairs continued to discuss the intricacies of the two murders, blaming everyone who had any connection whatsoever with the victims.

"Okay, okay, let me get this straight," summarized MacNab, consulting his notes. "You think maybe Larry de la Roque is the guy we're after. Managed to sneak out of the hospital. Or maybe Smathers. Something about plagiarism. Or maybe the butch auto detailer, who had a fight with Bateman, whom she'd never met. Or maybe those dope dealers, the Corsican brothers. Or that set-back man you ran into one night. Or maybe Steve hit him on the head because he's irritable. Or maybe Mrs. Bateman did it and welded him in there, and went out to the wrecking yard and killed Fast Eddie because he knew something about it. Or maybe Mrs. Scroggins because she knows how to weld. And now you're saying Phil was in some deal with Eddie. They killed Bateman and then Phil killed Eddie. Have I missed anyone? How about that dog at the wrecking yard. What's his name?"

"Corky," said Charles.

"You can have a lawyer anytime, Dr. Carstairs," said MacNab. "You know that, don't you? We've told you several times, haven't we?"

"Look, I don't know who killed anyone," said Charles. "I just know I didn't. So someone else must have. It's that simple."

"We're not getting anywhere," said Lukowski, pulling at his tie, which was already loosened. "The point is, we saw you standing there, right over the dead man. The jackstands had been knocked out somehow, and you were running away from the scene. We have to know what happened." He leaned over the table, shoving aside some rancid-looking fries on a crumpled piece of waxed paper. "You're a scholar. You study the workings of society. The workings of society won't work if people go around killing other people. Surely you see that."

"This guy's wearing me out," muttered MacNab. "Listen, if you ask for a lawyer, Dr. Carstairs, maybe he can arrange bail and get you home tomorrow."

There was a knock at the door to the interview room.

MacNab went to it and consulted in low tones with a young woman.

Lukowski looked across at Charles. "I bet it was just hell, not getting tenure," he said. "Naturally you were upset. You went home, pigged out on a lot of junk food, watched some horrible movies."

Carstairs seemed to bristle. "Everyone has bad days," he said. "It doesn't mean I killed Dr. Bateman."

MacNab came back into the room and beckoned to Lukowski. Outside the room, MacNab said, "That book-keeper of his just called. Says if we go right over to the shop we've got a good chance of catching the killer red-handed. She says there's some evidence there on the premises the killer will be after."

"Oh, yeah?"

"Sounds to me like she's cooking up some more of this phony stuff the professor's been trying to sell."

"Listen," said Lukowski. "We've got him clean on that Eddie guy. But I still can't put it all together on Bateman. There are too many loose ends. Cars disappearing. Body welded in there. It's too squirrelly. The only way we may be able to nail him for the first murder is if we can prove he's trying to frame someone else."

"Just what I've been thinking. It even occurred to me we should take him along to see what this broad's cooked up. He may say and do something stupid."

"So what else is new?" said Lukowski wearily. "Okay. Let's go. He won't give us any trouble, will he?"

"We'll keep the cuffs on him," said MacNab. "He's worn me out," he added. "I can't believe I have to keep encouraging him to get a lawyer so we can go home and stop listening to his theories. Get this. We're supposed to meet in that crazy Mrs. Scroggins's garage."

Lukowski looked thoughtful. "I guess they've got her roped in somehow in whatever scam they're trying to pull. It's pathetic, using a poor old crazy woman like that."

"Let's face it," said MacNab. "This Carstairs has that poor beatnik girl in love with him. Now she's going to perjure herself for him."

"Well, let's go and get it over with," said Lukowski.

Carstairs seemed optimistic in the car on the way over. The detectives hadn't told him much, but at the mention of Sylvia Snow's name he assured them that his bookkeeper was a very bright woman who would be sure to shed some light on a puzzling situation.

"Sylvia," he cried, clumsily lurching toward her with his hands cuffed behind him.

"Oh, Charles," she whispered. "I've been so worried about you. Are you all right? You should have called a lawyer."

"She's got that right," muttered MacNab.

"What's *he* doing here?" said Mrs. Scroggins sharply.

"Shh!" said Sylvia. They were standing in Mrs. Scroggins's garage, which was filled with rusty garden tools, rotting wicker furniture, a croquet set, and a vintage Packard Lukowski couldn't help but admire. He wondered how much Mrs. Scroggins would let it go for. He might be able to make a good deal, but he repressed the unworthy thought.

"Come over here," said Sylvia Snow, beckoning them to the garage door, which had a row of dusty small windowpanes along the top. They looked out on the alley behind Cosmo's Car Center.

"I feel like a damn fool," MacNab said to Lukowski.

"Of course it's just a theory," said Sylvia. "But if I'm right, there are only two things the murderer thinks would link the killing to this place. Fast Eddie, and he's already taken care of that, and the weapon."

"The weapon!" said MacNab and Lukowski in unison.

"Shh!" repeated Sylvia. "Watch."

They stood in a row, looking out the windows. A figure was fumbling under the garbage can, where the spare key was kept.

"I told you not to leave the key out there any more," said Charles sharply to Sylvia.

"Charles, just shut up," she whispered.

They heard the creaking sound of the rear door being raised.

"Give him about thirty seconds," said Sylvia. "Then go in." A light went on in the shop.

MacNab and Lukowski gave it about fifteen seconds, then, instructing the two women to stay behind, they went, with Charles, into the shop. The two women ignored their instructions and followed.

Lukowski wasn't sure who the middle-aged man with the shock of red hair was. All he could see was that the man wore a long red rubber glove and was fishing around in a big drum of some kind of fluid. He had just retrieved a large wrench and was holding it up like a fishing trophy when he perceived he wasn't alone.

"Uncle Cosmo!" said Charles. "In disguise."

"This isn't a disguise," said the man indignantly. "This is a fine custom hairpiece. I've always wanted a nice piece and now I can afford one."

"That's the weapon," said Sylvia breathlessly. "One of our mechanics found it in there this morning, but Cosmo didn't know that. That's why I put it back in there. And he came back to get it. He killed Bateman with that wrench. Then he threw the wrench in there. A perfect place to clean a bloody weapon, by the way. Then he threw Bateman's groceries in the dumpster."

"Who the hell is she?" demanded Uncle Cosmo.

"We know about those groceries," said MacNab.

"You do?" said Charles.

"And then he towed the professor's car to the airport," continued Sylvia. "So that when he vanished it would look voluntary."

"So why would he leave the body right here in the shop?" said MacNab sarcastically. He'd wait to tell the girl about Cosmo's alibi later. Let her show them what she had.

"But that's just it," said Sylvia. "He didn't. I just figured it out today, after talking to Phil. Cosmo welded the body in there, and he towed it to Elwood's. He put it in the line of cars to be crushed. His tow truck was seen there the very Saturday night. And it was easy for him to get into the wrecking yard. Corky, the guard dog, was his old pet. That detective Ferguson told us all about the layout."

"That would account for the welding," said Charles thoughtfully. "Otherwise the crusher could pop the trunk open and the body would fall out."

"Let me finish," said Sylvia. "What Cosmo didn't realize was that Elwood had a dishonest employee."

"Fast Eddie?" said Charles. Lukowski watched him. If he had come up with this story with the girl, he was a damn good actor. He looked genuinely confused.

"That's right. Ferguson, the private eye, stumbled onto it. Elwood was scrapping everything in sight. Fast Eddie stole a car or two destined for the crusher, fixed it up, with Phil's help, and sold it. He stole Ferguson's car. And he stole that Volvo Cosmo put in line to be scrapped."

"I bet Uncle Cosmo smashed the windshield just to

make it look like more of a basket case," said Charles. "So that it would get cubed."

"What he didn't know was that Fast Eddie would steal the car and bring it right back to Cosmo's. For Phil to work on. Where we discovered it." Sylvia looked very pleased with herself.

"Hey," said Charles, right on cue, Lukowski thought. "Eddie called here right after we discovered the body. Phil told him the cops were all over the place and that we'd found a body in a Volvo."

"So Eddie lay low. He couldn't get involved. He'd stolen the car," said Sylvia.

"Who the hell is this woman? And are these guys cops? Why are you wearing handcuffs?" Uncle Cosmo was getting red in the face.

"I'm Sylvia Snow. The bookkeeper your nephew hired. And yes, these are police officers."

"Are you getting all this?" said MacNab to Lukowski.

"Sort of," said Lukowski. "So far it's almost making sense."

"But why?" said Charles, looking over at Uncle Cosmo, a pathetic figure in the reddish toupee.

"I think I know that too," said Sylvia.

"Hold on," bellowed Cosmo. "I wasn't anywhere near this place. I was at a bank seminar."

"So you say," said Sylvia with a smirk. "Got any witnesses?"

"Yes, he does," said Lukowski simply.

"Oh," said Sylvia. She looked genuinely puzzled.

"Lock him up," said Mrs. Scroggins. "Throw away the key."

"Then it must have something to do with that lipstick," said Sylvia thoughtfully. "It's the only detail that doesn't make sense. That and the fact that Uncle Cosmo has an alibi.''

''What was the motive you came up with?'' said Charles. ''Why in God's name would Uncle Cosmo want to kill Dr. Bateman? Other than that he was a pompous creep.''

''I never killed Bateman,'' said Cosmo firmly.

''The hell you say,'' snarled Mrs. Scroggins.

''I've learned a lot about your uncle by going over his books,'' said Sylvia. ''Greed. It's all over his business dealings. But stupid greed. He wasn't willing to work out his business problems, he always went for the quick killing.''

''Get to the point,'' said Charles irritably.

''The lottery ticket,'' said Sylvia. ''It was Saturday, when the winning lottery number is announced. Bateman had a winning lottery ticket. Cosmo killed him and took it. Then tried to make the body disappear. He would have succeeded too, if Fast Eddie hadn't been a crook just like Cosmo.''

''But Mr. Sweeney had an alibi,'' said Lukowski patiently. ''Besides,'' he added, ''Bateman was killed before the winner was announced at six o'clock. He was due home to dress for dinner at five.''

''That explains it, sort of,'' said Sylvia.

''Unless Cosmo here found Bateman dead around six, after that bank workshop,'' said MacNab.

''And rolled the body,'' said Lukowski. ''Interesting.''

''Wait a minute. Wait a minute,'' said Uncle Cosmo. ''I won that fair and square. Hell, I've been buying lottery tickets for years. It was about time my number came up.''

''Okay, try this,'' said Sylvia slowly. ''Uncle Cosmo comes back from the bank thing. Finds Bateman dead in his shop. Phil had left it open and Bateman could have come in to wait for Cosmo. Someone killed him, then

Cosmo discovered him. He probably intended to call the police. But he checked the victim's wallet first. He found some cash, and the lottery ticket. The announcement is made at six. There's a TV on the premises. Cosmo decides to keep the ticket, but he knows he can't keep it if it's suspected it was Bateman's. So he makes it look like the crime never happened. He arranges to make the body disappear permanently. Tows Bateman's car to the airport, as I said. Dumps Bateman's groceries in the dumpster and drops the bloody wrench in the cold tank, where it would be cleaned. It would have worked. Bateman's body would never have been found. His car would show up at the airport. The police would have said he left town on his own. Just another middle-aged man snapping.''

"If that were true," said Cosmo, "why would I go to all that trouble, towing cars around and welding and stuff? Why wouldn't I just take the ticket?''

"It wouldn't have been too smart," said Lukowski. "Questions would have been asked if you won six million dollars on the same day a body was found in your shop. After all, those tickets can be sourced to the place they were sold.''

"What about Fast Eddie?" said MacNab.

"When Cosmo called this morning, he learned that Mrs. Scroggins had seen Fast Eddie deliver that car," said Sylvia. "He couldn't afford to have anyone know the way the car got here. It would be traced right back to the shop. He would do anything to protect his income from the lottery.''

"Weren't you in Alaska?" said Charles to his uncle. He seemed to be reeling. "Where were you really?''

"Oh, he was in Alaska," said Sylvia. "He called collect to establish an alibi. Then he came right down here to confront Eddie. To find out what he knew. I called the airlines. It takes three hours and twenty minutes to fly down here from Anchorage. Cosmo probably called from the airport. It was probably true that he first learned that Bateman's body had been discovered in a Seattle newspaper on the Vegas–Anchorage flight. As soon as he landed, he called to find out whether he was in danger of losing his money. He realized that the wrench, which meant nothing if the body were gone, took on new significance when a body had been found there. Charles even mentioned the police were looking for a tool that matched the dent in Bateman's skull. And he found out that Fast Eddie had been moving the car around and could put two and two together.''

"The little son-of-a-bitch tried to shake me down,'' burst out Uncle Cosmo. He began to weep. "He wanted it all. All my money. He said he could prove I killed Bateman. But I never did. I swear to God. He was dead when I got here at six.''

"So you did roll him for that lottery ticket?'' said MacNab, advancing toward him.

"I never did,'' said Cosmo. "It's mine. Fair and square.''

"And you did kill Fast Eddie,'' said Lukowski indignantly. "It was so easy. Just kick out those jackstands.''

"He could have jumped the fence,'' said Charles softly, looking at his uncle in horror. "To avoid Elwood.''

"But who killed Bateman?'' said MacNab.

"I'm not absolutely sure,'' said Sylvia. "But it had to be a woman.''

They all turned to her. "What?'' said Lukowski.

"He didn't go on those errands alone,'' said Sylvia. "There was a lipstick in those groceries. No woman sends

193

a man out to buy a lipstick. The shade is too important. You have to be sure of the color.''

"The junkman said *his* wife didn't like the color," said Charles in awe. He was staring at Sylvia.

"Bateman wasn't alone," she continued. "He was waiting for Uncle Cosmo with a woman. The woman who'd bought that lipstick. Maybe they quarreled. It doesn't seem as if she had planned it. She hit him with a wrench. And left."

"Probably his wife," said MacNab. "You know my number one rule of homicide."

"What?" said Charles.

"When you find a dead body," quoted Lukowski distractedly, "ask yourself if that body is married. Remember what the woman up at the college told us? Mrs. Bateman had her license suspended. She had to have her husband drive her around on errands."

"Why did she kill her husband?" asked Charles of no one in particular.

"I think she has a temper," said Lukowski. He thought about that shard of china in her welcome mat. The one that came from the vase on the mantel. She'd said the cat knocked it down. If that were true, why was there a piece of it on the front doormat? Only because she'd thrown it at someone leaving the house. Probably in a domestic dispute. As to what they could have quarreled about, waiting here at Cosmo's Car Center, it was pure speculation, but Lukowski had a theory. The secretary at the university had told them that Bateman hadn't wanted his wife to come with him to the dinner in his honor. Afraid she'd drink too much. But Mrs. Bateman had sounded like she wanted to go. The mayor was going to be there, she'd said. And it was very elegant. Black tie. They might have been fighting about that.

He looked over at his partner. "Think Mrs. Bateman's good for it?" he said.

MacNab shrugged. "All circumstantial. And think what a good defense attorney could do with all these lowlifes hanging around this garage."

"That's for sure," said Mrs. Scroggins.

"Perhaps it can be proved somehow," said Sylvia, furrowing her smooth brow.

"Perhaps," said Lukowski. He didn't see how. There was no physical evidence linking her to the crime.

"She must have killed Eddie too," said Uncle Cosmo optimistically.

"Sorry, Cosmo," said MacNab. "We've had a surveillance on her for the past few days. I just got a report from the men in the field before I came over here. We've got a couple of police officers who'll swear she never left the house."

"You can't get me," said Cosmo. "You can't. I can afford the best criminal lawyers in the country."

"Not any more you can't," said Sylvia. "That wasn't your lottery ticket."

"I don't get it," said Mrs. Scroggins. "How many people did he kill?"

"It's very simple," said Sylvia. "It seems complicated when you don't know what really happened, but it's basically simple. One. Someone, possibly Mrs. Bateman, killed the professor and left the scene. Two. Cosmo arrives at six, takes the lottery ticket from Dr. Bateman's wallet, and does what he can to make it look as if the murder never happened. Three. Eddie unwittingly returns the body to the scene in that old car. You saw that, Mrs. Scroggins. Four.

Cosmo learns the body made it back here. He comes down to clean up some more. He kills Fast Eddie, who may well have tried to blackmail him, and he goes for the weapon. Got it?''

Mrs. Scroggins looked a little vague, but she said with spirit, ''Well, I'm glad the old bastard will finally be going to jail. I've known about him for years.''

The policemen took the handcuffs off Charles and put them on Cosmo. As they led him away, Sylvia went up to Cosmo and put a dollar bill in his shirt pocket.

''What was that about?'' said Charles.

''You never read that contract you signed with your uncle,'' she said. ''He gave you his business all right. For the sum of one dollar. I bet you never paid it. Now you do own the business.''

''Doesn't your mind ever stop?'' he asked her.

Mrs. Scroggins followed Cosmo and the policemen outside, obviously satisfied that her old nemesis was facing justice at last.

''Sometimes it does,'' Sylvia said, walking toward him. ''Sometimes it just cranks to a halt, and my feelings take over. Not very often though.'' She put her arms around him. ''I'm glad you're safe,'' she said, her head falling to his shoulder. ''I was going crazy thinking they'd locked you up. I'm glad you're safe now so I can stop thinking.''

''No more detecting for a while, then?'' said Charles softly. He stroked her hair.

''Not until Saturday,'' she replied.

The following Saturday, a very reluctant Charles stood with Sylvia at the bus stop in front of Cosmo's Car Center.

''This is ridiculous,'' he said. ''The police can handle this.''

"I'm sorry," said Sylvia. "It's just that she had to have got home somehow. And I like to finish what I've started."

"Well I've started a carb job in there, and I'd like to finish it up. You know I hate working on Saturdays."

A bus pulled up in front of them with a horrible squeal. Thing needed a brake job badly, thought Charles.

Sylvia, checking her wristwatch, climbed aboard, and Charles followed. They deposited their quarters in the fare box. A bored-looking driver gave them a curt nod.

"Excuse me," began Sylvia. "Is this your regular route?"

"Yes, it is. Don't worry, I know the way."

Charles was embarrassed. Why had he come along?

Sylvia continued. "I wonder if you remember picking up a woman here on the twelfth? It was a Saturday. She was an attractive woman—"

"Blond? Late forties? Hair hanging down over half her face? Got on at this stop?" said the driver.

"Yes, yes," said Sylvia enthusiastically.

"Nope. Never saw her." The bus driver pulled into traffic. Charles lurched against Sylvia, who grabbed the fare box to steady herself.

"Then how do you know what she looked like?" said Sylvia indignantly.

"Because the cops asked me all about her," he said. He pointed to a sign above him. *Please Avoid Unnecessary Conversation With Operator* it read.

Charles led a dejected Sylvia to a seat. "I told you the police are on this," he said.

"He didn't have to be so surly," said Sylvia. "It's a wonder he ever got that courtesy patch he's wearing."

"Excuse me," said a voice behind them. They turned to see a small woman with an unlikely-looking coiffure—it was probably a wig—of dense red curls. She had a sharp little face behind old-fashioned cat-eye glasses. "Did I hear you say you were looking for a woman who got on at this stop a couple of weeks ago? Blond. Good-looking."

"That's right," said Sylvia.

"I remember her," said the woman. "That lady sat next to me. She had a lot of questions about how to transfer to Laurelhurst."

"Do you think you could identify her again?" asked Sylvia breathlessly.

Charles wondered if she could. Eyewitness identification, he knew, was often unreliable. Any attractive blond woman in her late forties could have taken this bus at some time or other when this woman was a passenger.

"How come you remember her?" said Charles.

"Well," said the woman. "She had real nice things. A diamond ring I'd guess was half a carat. Real expensive wool slacks. The sweater was cashmere. I run into a lot of nice things in my line."

"Oh?" said Sylvia.

"Yeah. I'm a hotel maid. Down at the Olympic. I come off shift every Saturday at the same time and take this bus home. That's why I know when it was."

"So you remembered her by her clothes," said Sylvia.

"That's right. It seemed so strange that a careful dresser like that would have blood all over her sleeve."

EPILOGUE

Six months later, early one morning, Charles came into the shop waving an envelope. He was eager to give Sylvia the news.

Sylvia, behind the counter and wearing a Peruvian sweater with llamas and a Guatemalan skirt, spoke before he had a chance.

"A postcard from your uncle. I hope it's okay I read it." Their relationship was now intimate enough for Sylvia to read a postcard. "He wants us to hire one of the guys in his class. A sexual psychopath."

Uncle Cosmo's defense had been that any normal person would have killed a loser like Fast Eddie to protect six million dollars. The jury of ten housewives, a retired postal worker, and a Boeing engineer, had thought otherwise. Uncle Cosmo was now serving fifteen years to life in the state penitentiary, but had adjusted well and was teaching a class in auto mechanics. "He says the boys there keep a real clean shop," she added.

"A sexual psychopath! I've got enough problems." Charles was indignant. "Listen, it's a good thing I went home and checked on my mail, because . . ." He was whispering in the mistaken belief that the mechanics were unaware that he spent most nights at Sylvia's killim-festooned apartment these days.

"And guess what else?" interrupted Sylvia, waving the morning paper at him. "There's a story on Mrs. Bateman in here. Take a look."

There was a photograph of Mrs. Bateman in handcuffs and the headline: *Slayer Sues Therapist. My Shrink Made Me Do It.* "And listen to this," continued Sylvia breath-lessly. " 'Elizabeth Bateman, who pled guilty to manslaugh-ter in the bludgeoning death of her husband, Professor Roland Bateman, filed a civil suit in Superior Court today against her psychiatrist, Dr. James Thorndyke. The suit alleges that Dr. Thorndyke encouraged Mrs. Bateman to express her anger. The suit seeks one million dollars in compensatory damages for the loss of Mrs. Bateman's freedom for five years, and for the loss of support and companionship of her spouse, the late Dr. Bateman. In addition, Mrs. Bateman is seeking damages of an addi-tional six million, to make up for the loss of Dr. Bateman's lottery winnings. Because killers cannot inherit from their victims, the State of Washington refused to disburse the funds.

" 'According to Mrs. Bateman's attorney, Dr. Thorndyke told his patient to express her rage, and to practice letting out her feelings by beating up on pillows, screaming, kicking objects, and beating the ground with a broom. Mrs. Bateman struck her husband with a large wrench during an argument in an auto repair shop, killing him.

The attorney added that expert witnesses for Mrs. Bateman will testify that new studies of anger indicate that habitual release of anger increases rather than lessens feelings of anger in susceptible individuals.' "

Sylvia looked up at him. "What do you think about that!" she exclaimed.

"Oh, never mind about *her*," said Charles impatiently. "Look what I got in the mail. It's an offer from that liberal arts college in South Dakota. They're offering me a full professorship. *And* tenure."

"Oh," said Sylvia, letting the newspaper fall to the counter.

"I don't know what to do," said Charles. "I've been thinking about it in the car on the way over. I don't know how it will feel to leave the business. And you. Especially you." He smiled at her. "I suppose you don't want to move to South Dakota," he said wistfully, coming to her side, kicking the door to the shop closed and putting his arms around her.

"I don't know," she said, gazing up solemnly at him. "How much are they offering? We can compare it with my net income projections for this place."

"You do that," said Charles tenderly. "Can you combine the data with the projections you're doing on our tax picture if we get married?"

"Oh, the hell with it," she said, kissing him. "I think we should get married anyway. By the way," she added, nuzzling his neck, "Mrs. Colman called and she loved the work we did on her car. She's telling all her friends about us."

The shop door burst open and Steve came in. "No wonder this place is so fucked up," he said. "Instead of

concentrating on business you're just thinking about f—"
but he never finished his sentence because Charles had
made his hand into a fist and planted it on Steve's jaw,
sending him backward into the coffee machine.

About the Author

K. K. BECK has given us two previous period novels about that charming flapper, Iris Cooper, in DEATH IN A DECK CHAIR and MURDER IN A MUMMY CASE. She is also the author of the mysteries YOUNG MRS. CAVENDISH AND THE KAISER'S MEN, THE BODY IN THE VOLVO and UNWANTED ATTENTIONS.

To the delight of her readers, K. K. Beck has left her former career in advertising to become a full-time novelist. She lives in Seattle with her husband and three children.